Aung San Suu Kyi

Women Changing the World

Aung San Suu Kyi
Standing Up for Democracy in Burma

Rigoberta Menchú
Defending Human Rights in Guatemala

Máiread Corrigan and Betty Williams
Making Peace in Northern Ireland

Advisory Board for Women Changing the World

Aung San Suu Kyi

Standing Up for Democracy in Burma

Bettina Ling

The Feminist Press
at The City University of New York
New York

Published by The Feminist Press at The City University of New York
City College, Wingate Hall, Convent Avenue at 138th Street, New York, NY 10031

First edition, 1999

Library of Congress Cataloging-in-Publication Data

Ling, Bettina.
    Aung San Suu Kyi : standing up for democracy in Burma / Bettina Ling.
        p.   cm. — (Women changing the world)
    Includes bibliographical references and index.
    Summary: A biography which traces the life of the Burmese
  political activist who was awarded the Nobel Peace Prize in 1991.
        ISBN 1-55861-196-7 (lib. bdg.). - ISBN 1-55861-197-5 (pbk.)
        1. Aung San Suu Kyi—Juvenile literature. 2. National League for Democracy (Burma)—
Juvenile literature. 3. Women political activists—Burma—Biography—Juvenile
literature. 4. Women political prisoners—Burma—Biography—Juvenile literature.
5. Democracy—Burma—Juvenile literature. 6. Burma—Politics and government—1988—Juvenile
literature.   [1. Aung San Suu Kyi. 2. Political activists. 3. Women—Biography.
4. Burma—Politics and government—1988] I. Title. II. Series.
DS530.53.A85L56   1999
959.105'092-dc21
[b]   98-44109
                                                                                              CIP
                                                                                              AC

The Feminist Press is grateful to the Ford Foundation for their generous support of our work. The Feminist Press is also grateful to Joanne Markell, Johnetta B. Cole, Florence Howe, Caroline Urvater, Genevieve Vaughan, Susan Weiler, Lynn Gernert, Patricia Wentworth, Mark Fagan, Judith Wit, and Lynn Birks for their generosity in supporting this publication.

Design by Dayna Navaro
Typesetting by CompuDesign

Printed on acid-free paper by RR Donnelley & Sons
Manufactured in Mexico

05   04   03   02   01   00   99   5   4   3   2   1

CONTENTS

WHAT DOES IT TAKE TO CHANGE THE WORLD?

Maybe this question sounds overwhelming. However, people who become leaders have all had to ask themselves this question at some point. They started finding answers by choosing how they would lead their lives every day and by creating their own opportunities to make a difference in the world. The anthropologist Margaret Mead said, "Never doubt that a small group of thoughtful, committed citizens can change the world; indeed it's the only thing that ever has." So let's look at some of the qualities possessed by people who are determined to change the world.

First, it takes vision. The great stateswoman and humanitarian Eleanor Roosevelt said, "You must do the thing you think you cannot do." People who change the world have the ability to see what is wrong in their society. They also have the ability to imagine something new and better. They do not accept the way things *are*—the "status quo"— as the only way things *must be* or *can be*. It is this vision of an improved world that inspires others to join leaders in their efforts to make change. Leaders are not afraid to be different, and the fear of failure does not prevent them from trying to create a better world.

Second, it takes courage. Mary Frances Berry, former head of the U.S. Commission on Civil Rights, said, "The time when you need to do something is when no one else is willing to do it, when people are saying it can't be done." People who change the world know that courage means more than just saying what needs to be changed. It means deciding to be active in the effort to bring about change—no matter what it takes. They know they face numerous challenges: they may be criticized, made fun of, ignored, alienated from their friends and family, imprisoned, or even killed. But even though they may sometimes feel scared, they continue to pursue their vision of a better world.

Third, it takes dedication and patience. The Nobel Prize–winning scientist Marie Curie said, "One never notices what has been done; one can only see what remains to be done." People who change the world understand that change does not happen overnight. Changing the world is an ongoing process. They also know that while what they do is important, change depends on what others do as well. Their original vision may transform and evolve over time as it interacts with the visions of others and as circumstances change. And they know that the job is never finished. Each success brings a new challenge, and each failure yet another obstacle to overcome.

Finally, it takes inspiration. People who change the world find strength in the experiences and accomplishments of others who came before them. Sometimes these role models are family members or personal friends. Sometimes they are great women and men who have spoken out and written about their own struggles to change the world for the better. Reading books about these people—learning about their lives and reading their own words—can be a source of inspiration for future world-changers. For example, when I was young, someone gave me a book called *Girls' Stories of Great Women,* which provided me with ideas of what women had achieved in ways I had never dreamed of and in places that were very distant from my small town. It helped me to imagine what I could do with my life and to know that I myself could begin working toward my goals.

This series of books introduces us to women who have changed the world through their vision, courage, determination, and patience. Their stories reveal their struggles as world-changers against obstacles such as poverty, discrimination, violence, and injustice. Their stories also tell of their struggles as women to overcome the belief, which still exists in most societies, that girls are less capable than boys of achieving high goals, and that women are less likely than men to become leaders. These world-changing women often needed even more vision and courage than their male counterparts, because as women they faced greater discrimination and resistance. They certainly needed more determination and patience, because no matter how much they proved themselves, there were always people who were reluctant to take their leadership and their achievements seriously, simply because they were women.

These women and many others like them did not allow these challenges to stop them. As they fought on, they found inspiration in women as well as men—their own mothers and grandmothers, and the great women who had come before them. And now they themselves stand as an inspiration to young women and men all over the world.

The women whose lives are described in this series come from different countries around the world and represent a variety of cultures. Their stories offer insights into the lives of people in varying circumstances. In some ways, their lives may seem very different from the lives of most people in the United States. We can learn from these differences as well as from the things we have in common. Women often share similar problems and concerns about issues such as violence in their lives and in the world, or the kind of environment we are creating for the future. Further, the qualities that enable women to become leaders, and to make positive changes, are often the same worldwide.

The first set of books in this series tells the stories of four women who have won what might be called humanity's highest honor: the Nobel Peace Prize.

The Nobel Peace Prize recognizes leaders who try to improve their societies using peaceful means. These leaders have faced many different kinds of challenges and have responded to them in different ways. But one goal they all share is to promote "human rights"—the basic rights to which all human beings are entitled.

In 1948, the United Nations adopted the *Universal Declaration of Human Rights,* which outlines the rights of all people to freedom from slavery and torture, and to freedom of movement, speech, religion, and assembly, as well as rights of all people to social security, work, health, housing, education, culture, and citizenship. Further, it states that all people have the equal right to all these human rights, "without distinction of any kind such as race, color, sex, language . . . or other status."

In the United States, many of these ideas are not new to us. Some of them can be found in the first ten amendments to the U.S. Constitution, known as the Bill of Rights. Yet these ideals continually face many challenges, and they must be defended and expanded by every generation. They have been tested in this country, for example, by the Civil Rights movement to end racial discrimination and the movement to bring about equal rights for women. They continue to be tested even today by various individuals and groups who are fighting for greater equality and justice.

All over the world, women and men work for and defend the common goal of human rights for all. In some places these rights are severely violated.

Tradition and prejudice as well as social, economic, and political interests often exclude women, in particular, from benefitting from these basic rights. Over the past decade, women around the world have been questioning why "women's rights" and women's lives have been deemed secondary to "human rights" and the lives of men. As a result, an international women's human rights movement has emerged, with support from organizations such as the Center for Women's Global Leadership, to challenge limited ideas about human rights and to alert all nations that "women's rights are human rights."

The following biography is the true story of a woman overcoming incredible obstacles—economic hardship, religious persecution, political oppression, and even the threat of violence and death—in order to peacefully achieve greater respect for human rights in her country. I am sure that you will find her story inspiring. I hope it also encourages you to join in the struggle to demand an end to all human rights violations—regardless of sex, race, class, or culture—throughout the world. And perhaps it will motivate you to become someone who just might change the world.

Charlotte Bunch
Founder and Executive Director
Center for Women's Global Leadership
Rutgers University

You can help to change the world now by establishing goals for yourself personally and by setting an example in how you live and work within your own family and community. You can speak out against unfairness and prejudice whenever you see it or hear it expressed by those around you. You can join an organization that is fighting for something you believe in, volunteer locally, or even start your own group in your school or neighborhood so that other people who share your beliefs can join you. Don't let anything or anyone limit your vision. Make your voice heard with confidence, strength, and dedication . . . and start changing the world today.

"Violence is its own worst enemy, and fearlessness is the sharpest weapon against it."

—Professor Francis Sejersted
Chairman of the
Norwegian Nobel Committee

Aung San Suu Kyi, courageous and determined leader of the National League for Democracy, has campaigned for democracy in Burma since 1988.

Chapter 1
A WOMAN OF COURAGE

Daw Suu stood in the sweltering heat of the Burmese evening, calmly facing the six soldiers. The military men were kneeling in the road with their rifles aimed at her. They were just waiting for the orders from their commander to shoot.

Just moments before, Aung San Suu Kyi (pronounced Awng San Su Chee) and some of her supporters had been walking down the middle of the road, returning from a small town where she had given a political speech to rally the citizens. Suddenly, a military jeep pulled in front of them. A squad of soldiers jumped from the jeep, knelt down, and prepared to fire on the group. An army captain shouted at Daw Suu and her supporters to get off the road. He said the soldiers would fire on them if they kept walking down the middle of the road.

Daw Suu called back to the captain that they would walk down the *side* of the road. She remained characteristically calm and polite, despite her dangerous position. The captain said they would shoot them even if they walked on the side of the road. She knew that the army and the government hated her. She decided that maybe the military men wanted to shoot her, regardless of where she walked. She motioned for the others with her to move away, and then she marched right up to the soldiers. She was not worried about her own safety. After all there was no point: If the governing military wanted to do anything to harm her, they could do it anytime they liked. They controlled the country and its citizens.

She stood defiantly as everyone waited to see what would happen. Her body was rigid and unbending. She knew if she gave in to this intimidation, then she would go on being intimidated. She later said in an interview, "I thought, what does one do? Does one turn back or keep going? My thought was, one doesn't turn back in a situation like this." She felt no fear. The soldiers cocked their guns. The seconds ticked by and tensions mounted. The approaching nightfall did little to cool the temperature raised during the day by the searing sun. But Daw Suu remained calm as she stared at the soldiers. Suddenly, the army major in command rushed up and gave an order for the soldiers to lower their guns. Daw Suu and her group walked through the still-kneeling soldiers. Once again she had refused to be intimidated by the tactics of the military government. Once again she had demonstrated her commitment and courage.

Aung San Suu Kyi—or Suu to family, Daw Suu to friends—was campaigning with other members of her political party, the National League for Democracy, or NLD, when this confrontation occurred in April 1989. They were preparing for an upcoming election in the small nation of Burma, in southeast Asia.

The struggle for democracy in Burma had a long history. In 1962, General Ne Win and his Burma Socialist Program Party seized control of Burma's government in a military coup. This was the beginning of Ne Win's military dictatorship, which would last for the next twenty-six years. Since then the Burmese people have lived in fear and poverty under a government regime that has illegally killed or imprisoned thousands of people.

In early 1988, the country of Burma was put under martial law because thousands of students and other citizens had started demonstrating in the streets. They were protesting their terrible living conditions and miserable economy brought about by General Ne Win and his Burma Socialist Program Party. During his dictatorship, Burma went from one of the most prosperous, educated countries in Asia to one of the poorest and most isolated.

At first Daw Suu was only an observer of the political conflicts, but she joined the struggle for freedom after an incident in which hundreds of unarmed protesters were gunned down by the military during a nonviolent demonstration. Daw Suu and her political party became the first ray of hope for the oppressed Burmese people.

Emerging as a natural leader, Daw Suu led nonviolent protests and gave numerous inspiring speeches across the country. She cofounded the National League for Democracy (NLD) to run against the military party, the State Law and Order Restoration Council (SLORC) in the 1990 elections. She became a rallying point for the people as she encouraged them to fight for their rights and a free democratic government.

The SLORC military in turn harassed Daw Suu and her supporters, and then placed her under arrest. She was imprisoned in her own home for six years, and during that time she was not allowed to see anyone. For over two years she didn't even see her husband and two sons.

While she was held under house arrest, Daw Suu

and her NLD political party won control of the government by a landslide victory. SLORC refused to recognize the results of the election and has never turned over the government to the legally elected NLD party.

Throughout the period Daw Suu was under arrest, SLORC let her know that she could have her freedom—but she would have to leave the country and would never be allowed to return. But Daw Suu was loyal to the Burmese people and their struggle. She refused her own freedom because she would never abandon the citizens of Burma.

Daw Suu quietly and bravely defied the SLORC government during her period of captivity. She smuggled out speeches and writings to keep the voice of Burma heard throughout the world. Her courageous fight for freedom has brought attention to Burma from countries and human rights groups around the globe. Because of her efforts, Daw Suu has been recognized with over thirty prestigious prizes and honors, including the 1991 Nobel Peace Prize.

SLORC released Aung San Suu Kyi in 1995, yet she is still a "prisoner in her own country," because the government will never let her return to Burma if she leaves. She lives at all times with the threat of re-arrest and with the possibility that she could be assassinated by people loyal to the SLORC government. Still Daw Suu fearlessly continues to make optimistic speeches to the Burmese citizens to buoy their spirits, and to speak out and write about the abuses in her country.

It is Daw Suu's goal to bring democracy to Burma and to restore Burma's reputation as a country of beauty rather than turmoil; a country of educated citizens rather than uneducated, impoverished individuals; a wealthy country with financial resources rather than a country of corruption and greed. She wants the Burmese citizens to live no longer in fear of imprisonment, torture, or death by their government. Daw Suu hopes that her personal courage and commitment will serve as an inspiration to the people of Burma. She hopes that by her example, the people will also become dedicated to the fight for a democratic government.

Chapter 2

A BURMESE CHILDHOOD

When Aung San Suu Kyi was born in Rangoon, Burma, in 1945, her father, General Aung San had just finished leading his country's military forces to victory in a war against Japan. Burma had succeeded at last in securing its independence from Japan. General Aung San returned from the war a beloved and respected national hero.

The triumph over the Japanese signaled the end of colonialism—the control of one nation over a dependent people or area—in Burma. Colonialism in Burma had begun over a century earlier, when the Burmese lost a series of wars against Great Britain. At that time, Great Britain was one of the most powerful countries in the world. Burma was added to a long list of British colonies, which included nearby India.

Under colonialism, a powerful foreign country controls the resources, the economy, and the government; the native inhabitants have little say in the control of their own country. British rule brought many changes to Burma, such as the development of the plentiful natural resources and increasing economic prosperity. But these changes did not benefit the native Burmese as much as they did the British colonists. Even the groups of people who came from other countries, like India and China, after the British takeover shared in the country's prosperity more than the Burmese people.

Where is Burma?

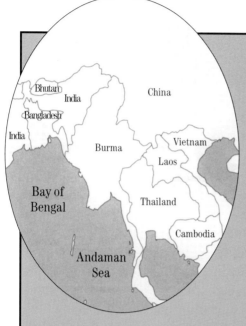

Only about the size of the state of Texas, Burma (now officially called Myanmar) is bordered by China, Laos, Thailand, Bangladesh, India, and the Andaman Sea and the Bay of Bengal.

The country has two dominant physical features: lowland areas and mountains. Down the center of Burma runs a core of lowland regions that are watered by two rivers, the Irrawaddy (the most important waterway in the country) and the Sittang. Another area of lowlands lies along the coasts. The remainder of the country is made up of rugged mountain and highland areas.

With its rich soil and tropical climate, Burma has abundant natural resources. Agriculture, forestry, and mining are the main elements of Burma's economy. The fertile soil makes it easy to grow rice and many kinds of food crops. The seas and rivers are full of a variety of fish. Tropical fruits are abundant, and the thick forests contain over 250 commercially useful kinds of timber and oil-bearing trees.

The ground in Burma has rich mineral deposits of lead, zinc, tin, coal, iron ore, natural gas, and petroleum. There are numerous deposits of precious stones such as rubies, sapphires, jade, and lapis lazuli. The oceans off Burma's coasts contain some of the world's most beautiful pearls.

British rule caused much of the Burmese culture to become submerged under the British culture. Among other things, the British tried to replace the Burmese languages with English. The British colonials also sought to change people's religious beliefs. Before the arrival of the British, most people in Burma practiced Buddhism. But during the period of colonialism, missionaries arrived who wanted to convert the people of Burma to the Christian religion.

Fortunately, the native Burmese culture was strong enough to stand up to colonial rule. The practice of Buddhism survived the period of British colonialism, as did the native languages—Burmese and several other ethnic languages. But the Burmese people would need to fight to regain the right of self-determination.

For years after the British takeover of Burma, many citizens were very unhappy with the Christian missionaries in their country. They also objected to the fact that the Burmese people were not the ones benefiting from the colony's growing prosperity. Like many countries—including the United States, which rose up against British colonial rule in 1776—Burma wanted its freedom and independence. Finally, in the early 1900s, Burmese resistance to the British rule began to flare up in many areas, and the different ethnic groups, once divided, started to band together.

In the 1930s, Burmese students organized stronger movements and formed political parties. When World War II broke out, these parties urged the Burmese not to support the British war efforts. The British retaliated by arresting many of these people, called nationalists, who were fighting for the independence of their country.

During this period, a group of young Burmese nationalists known as the "Thirty Comrades" secretly left the country and went to Japan to be given military training. One of the Thirty Comrades was a young man named Aung San—the father of Aung San Suu Kyi.

Japan was one of Britain's enemies in World War II, and the group had worked out a deal with the Japanese to help them take their country back from the British. The men received serious military train-

Who are the Burmese?

The Burmese people are the descendants of various ethnic groups that migrated to Burma in the ninth century. More than two-thirds of the people are ethnic Burmese, a race similar to the Tibetans and the Chinese. In addition, there are communities of immigrant Indians and Chinese in the cities and towns. Today Burma's native population falls into two broad groups—plains and hill people.

The main plains groups are the Burmese, Mon, Karen, and Rakhine peoples. The plains peoples reside in farming villages and have written languages and well-developed cultures.

The upland hill areas are populated by more than 100 different groups with separate cultures and languages. The largest are the hill Karen, the Shan, the Chin, and the Kachin. With the exception of the Shan, whose society and culture are like those of the plains peoples, the hill societies live in small mobile communities and support themselves through agriculture or as hunters.

Burmese is the national language, although local languages are used in the household and marketplace and in elementary schools. English is spoken among the educated, and the country contains a sizable number of speakers of Chinese.

ing and a few were chosen to command, including Aung San, who had emerged as a natural leader. In 1941 they marched back into Burma alongside the Japanese and drove the British out of their country.

But the joy of victory was short-lived as it became apparent that the Japanese wanted Burma for themselves. The Japanese turned out to be worse than the British, using torture and the threat of imprisonment to keep the Burmese people from rebelling as hundreds were used for forced labor.

General Aung San came to realize at this time that he had made a mistake when he asked Japan to assist Burma in gaining its independence from Britain. Quietly, he began to organize a resistance movement against the Japanese.

As the general tried to make plans for taking back the country from the Japanese, he also had to contend with in-fighting among the different political groups of Burma. He organized a new party called the AFO and managed the formidable task of uniting all the disagreeing forces. The general and his comrades then reunited with the British to fight against the Japanese. By June 1945, Burma had been taken back from the Japanese.

It was during this exciting and turbulent period that Aung San Suu Kyi came into the world on June 19, 1945. General Aung San had met Suu's mother, Ma Khin Kyi, in early 1942, while he was in a hospital where she was a senior staff nurse. Suu's parents were a good match. In the hospital, the general had gained a reputation as a quick-tempered, moody patient, and most of the hospital staff was frightened of him. Ma Khin Kyi was a strong woman and was not intimidated by him. She used patience and humor to calm the formidable man, and he, in turn, respected her strength, intelligence, and kindness.

During this time, many Burmese women held positions in the workplace and in politics, but they were prevented from achieving leadership roles. As in other parts of the world, women in Burma had formed their own groups in order to make their voices heard. Ma Khin Kyi had been an active member of a political group known as the Women's Freedom League, which took part in the independence movement against the British during the 1930s. She held the same passionate beliefs in Burmese independence as Aung San, and the two became fast friends. Their friendship grew quickly into love, and they were married in September 1942.

What is Burma's history?

Burma's multiethnic society reflects its long and varied history. Before the ninth century A.D., a succession of different ethnic groups of people migrated down the Irrawaddy River from Tibet and China. First came the Mon. A group known as the Pyu followed much later. The Burmans arrived in the mid-ninth century, absorbing the nearby Pyu and Mon communities. Later waves of migration brought in the Shan, Kachin, and Karen ethnic groups, who have all played a part in the country's development.

The first unified Burmese state was founded by King Anawrahta somewhere between 1044 and 1077. During his rule the country extended its political and religious ties overseas to Ceylon (now Sri Lanka) and fought off a Chinese invasion from the north. The Buddhist religion was introduced to Burma during this period.

In 1287, a group of Asiatic people known as Mongols invaded the country under the leadership of Kublai Khan, and the area was divided into different states ruled by various ethnic groups. A second unified dynasty was established in the late 1400s, and during the 1600s and early 1700s the British, Dutch, and French began business ventures on the Burmese coasts.

A new dynasty started in 1752, and the country was reunited under King Alaungpaya. During his rule and that of his successor, Burma extended its influence to India and fought off invasions by the Chinese, as well as British and French attempts to gain control of Burma.

The British started the First Anglo-Burmese War (1824–26), which left them in control of parts of Burma. They added to their territory in the Second and Third Anglo-Burmese Wars (1852–85), and Burma was completely annexed to British India by 1886. Thibaw, the last Burmese king, was exiled by the British, and the entire Burmese system of royalty was destroyed.

Aung San and Ma Khin Kyi settled down into a large comfortable house near Royal Lakes in Rangoon, the capital of Burma. Because of his family background, education, and personal success and popularity, the general belonged to Burma's upper class. This meant that the young couple had wealth and privileges not available to all Burmese. Two sons, Aung San U and Aung San Lin, were born before Suu joined the family. The newborn Suu had small, distinctive features and fine, dark hair. Of the three children, she looked the most like her father. Her name, Aung San Suu Kyi, means "a bright collection of strange victories."

While Ma Khin Kyi was busy with the care of three small children, she was also an important part of the many political gatherings that she and the general hosted in their home. The AFO had expanded into the Anti-Fascist People's Freedom League (AFPFL). Aung San and Ma Khin Kyi made their home the center of the discussions and planning meetings of this new political party.

The Japanese had been driven out of Burma, but some of the British military and political leaders still considered Burma to be a colony of the British Empire. But the Burmese people were determined to have their independence. General Aung San aided in

General Aung San and Ma Khin Kyi were married in 1942. Here they pose for their wedding photo.

working out a solution through diplomacy, rather than through more fighting.

The task was not easy. The Burmese had not governed themselves since the late 1800s. Now there were disagreements among the many political parties and the different ethnic groups about how they wanted to govern their country.

In January 1946, General Aung San organized the first All Burma Conference. Participants from fifteen political parties and representatives of many different

In 1941, General Aung San (left) met briefly with a Burmese cabinet member at the airport before he flew to London to sign a historic agreement with the British government that granted Burma its independence.

ethnic groups attended. One of the groups attending was the Women's Freedom League, the party to which Ma Khin Kyi had belonged a few years before.

The conference passed a number of resolutions toward forming a new government, including the guarantee that all men and women over the age of eighteen would have the right to vote. Burmese women would be participating in politics equally with men and the following year, at the 1947 Constituent Assembly, three women won seats in the election.

In the final months before the British pulled completely out of Burma, there was still dissension among the Burmese political parties. The general worked hard to unite the different groups, so they would be a unified country when their independence was complete. But General Aung San would never get to see Burma's final transition from foreign occupation to complete independence.

On July 19, 1947, General Aung San and six leaders of the AFPFL, including his own brother, were assassinated by a group of men with machine guns during a meeting of their executive council.

Suu was only two years old when her father was assassinated, and so she was too young to have really known him, but from her father's example she learned to be deeply devoted to the good of her country, even if it meant risking harm or death. From her mother she learned courage and forgiveness. Ma Khin Kyi never spoke with hatred of her husband's assassins and she did not speak of revenge. This had a powerful influence on young Suu, who learned never to hate anyone, not even those people who would hurt her the most.

In order to ensure that her children would know of their father's heritage, Ma Khin Kyi maintained

Ma Khin Kyi, Aung San Suu Kyi's mother, was as politically active as her husband and equally well-regarded by the Burmese.

close friendships and ties with the general's military and political comrades. Suu grew up in their company, listening to tales about her father and his history as a leader. Suu was strongly influenced by a childhood spent with many educated, experienced, interesting adults.

After the general's death, Ma Khin Kyi began a political career of her own. Burma had achieved complete independence in the spring of 1948, and the government was now run by the Anti-Fascist People's Freedom League. The first prime minister was a man named U Nu, who had been a close comrade of General Aung San. Ma Khin Kyi succeeded her husband as a member of Parliament in the new Burmese independent government. She soon became one of Burma's most outstanding women politicians.

In 1953 Ma Khin Kyi was appointed as the country's first minister of social welfare, an office of the government that provides help and services to people suffering from poverty and other hardships. She was instrumental in founding voluntary social welfare societies and getting women throughout the country to become active in the organizations.

Suu and her brothers had an upbringing that was traditionally Burmese. Children in Burma are raised with strict social and moral codes. Much effort goes into teaching them how to be well behaved and courteous. The Burmese believe strongly in showing consideration, generosity, and hospitality to other people, and special respect to older people. Ma Khin Kyi was very strict about bringing her children up with these traditional Burmese values.

At Suu's house, meals were special family occasions.

What's in a name?

The Burmese do not have a system of family names. Instead, each person is given a personal name, different from the others of the family. Daw, Ma, U, or Maung are used like Mr. or Ms. Age is a factor in deciding which title to use. Daw means aunt or madam or lady, and U means uncle or sir, and wouldn't be used for children. Maung means younger brother so it is used for a young boy, but when he is older he is referred to as Ko, which means older brother. Ma, which means sister, is used for girls and women. A person's position can affect their title. U is used for a man of important status; Daw is used for an adult woman of great status. Women do not change their names when they marry, but they may add a title like Daw.

The family would sit for long periods around the dinner table laughing and sharing conversation, almost always with a few invited guests there with the family. A traditional Burmese meal might consist of hot, spicy curries with rice—a staple on Burmese dining tables—fish, and a lot of vegetables. Or there might be steaming bowls of *mobinga*, a peppery fish stew, served with vegetable fritters, slices of fish cake, hard-boiled eggs, and a squeeze of lime.

Suu and her family dressed in the traditional Burmese clothing of the time. The main item of clothing for both men and women is called a *lungyi*, a long tube of cloth that is wrapped around the body and tucked in at the waist. The men would wear shirts or collarless fitted jackets with their *lungyis*, and the women would wear short, fitted tops. The women often wore coiled strands of sweet-smelling jasmine intertwined with their hair. Suu especially loved to wear flowers in the long black braids that fell down her back.

Both of Suu's parents were Buddhists, and she and her brothers were brought up in the Buddhist faith.

The family had a Buddhist altar in the house at which they prayed, meditated, and made offerings.

When Suu was very young, she shared a bedroom with her brother Aung San Lin. They were best friends and loved to play together. Suu was a bit of a tomboy, and she and Aung San Lin spent hours playing games outdoors on the extensive grounds of the family home.

Tragedy struck the family again when Suu was seven years old. Aung San Lin drowned while playing along the banks of a lake on the family's property. The death affected Suu Kyi deeply.

But Suu was her mother's daughter, and her strength helped her cope with her brother's death. She later said, in an interview for the book *The Voice of Hope*, "His death was a tremendous loss for me. At that time I felt enormous grief . . . but it was not something I couldn't cope with." Soon after Aung San Lin's death, the family moved to a new home beside Inya Lake in Rangoon; this house, too, was always filled with people.

Education played a major part in Suu's young life. In Burma there is a high respect placed on the value of learning. Both girls and boys are sent to school in Burma, unlike some Asian countries where it is not considered as important to educate women.

Because the Burmese also feel strongly that children should learn proper social and moral values, most of the books for young children were stories teaching them how to behave correctly in life. In these books, great emphasis is placed on showing compassion and loving kindness to other people.

Suu read these Burmese children's moral stories and much more. She discovered early in life that she had a passion for books. Her mother encouraged all the children to read by taking them to the library. When Suu was young, a great-aunt told her stories from the *Jakata*, which are tales about the Buddha's life. She explained the teachings of the religion to Suu using these stories.

When Suu was nine, a cousin gave her a copy of the story "The Blue Carbuncle" by Sir Arthur Conan Doyle. Suu fell in love with the famous literary detective Sherlock Holmes. Her love for mystery and detective stories was born, and she would carry it into adulthood.

Suu's mother was a strict parent, but also a warm and loving one. Her relationship with her daughter was quite formal. In Ma Khin Kyi's generation in Burma, there was a formality between younger and older people, even between mothers and daughters. Suu not only loved and respected her mother, but she was in awe of her mother's integrity, courage, and discipline. Ma Khin Kyi was a perfectionist, and highly disciplined. She expected her children to be the same.

Of course, Suu's mother was also a very busy woman. She was a single parent in an important government position, as well as the widow of the highly regarded Burmese hero. Yet Ma Khin Kyi was always patient if her daughter needed to talk or had questions. At night, when a tired Ma Khin Kyi returned from a long day of work, she would lie on her bed as the young Suu walked around and around it, peppering her mother with questions about all kinds of subjects. Ma Khin Kyi never asked her to stop, never said she was too tired to answer.

Ma Khin Kyi taught her children to respect the

Aung San Suu Kyi at about six years old. As a child, Suu loved to explore the outdoors and read Burmese folktales. Later, she loved mysteries—especially the ones involving the famous detective Sherlock Holmes.

values their father stood for, such as courage and determination. She also taught them her values: she strongly believed in serving others and gaining satisfaction from giving rather than taking. She believed in the importance of not being a coward, and she taught her children to face their fears head-on and conquer them. As a small child, Suu Kyi had been extremely afraid of the dark. She conquered her fear when she was twelve years old by forcing herself to go downstairs alone at night to get a glass of milk. She would then walk around in the dark rooms in order to get over her fear.

Suu's family taught her to be open-minded about religious beliefs. Although the family was Buddhist, Suu's maternal grandfather was a Christian. Suu often read the Bible to him in Burmese. He talked to her about the value of respecting other people's religious beliefs.

Throughout her childhood, Suu went through different periods deciding what she wanted to be when she grew up. The influence of seeing and talking to her father's old military comrades made her decide, at the age of ten, that she would go into the army. She thought that would be a most honorable way to serve her country. A few years later, Suu's love of books made her abandon the army idea and decide she would become a writer. At the age of twelve, Suu discovered the classics of Burmese literature. The tiny girl could be seen carrying a book with her wherever she went.

Although she was raised in a strict environment, Suu behaved like any normal child, sometimes getting into trouble for misbehaving. During her elementary school years, Suu didn't like to work or study. She wanted to play all the time, and would sometimes be scolded for hiding to avoid having to do her homework. As she grew older Suu proved to be an outstanding student, with a sharp intelligence and a talent for languages. She was always at the top of her class.

Through most of her school years, Suu lived the life of a happy and normal Burmese teenager, with nothing too out of the ordinary. Then, in 1960, her mother was appointed ambassador to India. She was the first woman in Burmese history to serve as the head of a diplomatic mission. Ma Khin Kyi resigned her post as minister of social welfare, and the family prepared to move to India. For the teenage Aung San Suu Kyi, an exciting new world was about to open up.

Chapter 3

EDUCATION IN MANY COUNTRIES

Fifteen-year-old Suu and her family moved into a large house with a beautiful garden in New Delhi, India. Her older brother, Aung San U, went off to college in England to study electrical engineering. Although she had never lived here before, this country was not unfamiliar to Suu. India was a neighbor, and there were many Indian people living in Burma. Some of Suu's friends at school in Burma had been of Indian heritage.

Suu continued her high school education at the Convent of Jesus and Mary. At first she had not wanted to move to India and leave her friends back in Burma. But she gained a new group of Indian friends. Her mother made sure that Suu was also engaged in activities outside of school that would expose her to many different kinds of experiences. She took lessons in horseback riding, piano, and Japanese flower arranging. At these lessons she met and became friends with the children of Indian diplomatic officials and politicians.

Suu also assisted her mother in some of her ambassadorial duties, including entertaining important people from other countries at both diplomatic and personal social functions. Ambassadors are the official representatives of their government in all matters of state, and they act to promote and protect the nation they represent. They carry out foreign policies of a country, and serve as government repre-

Aung San Suu Kyi with her mother and brother Aung San U. Suu was very close to her brothers when she was growing up. The death of her brother Aung San Lin when she was seven years old deeply affected her.

sentatives at state functions, peace-keeping negotiations, foreign and economic meetings, and important social occasions such as state dinners. Her mother's position as ambassador exposed Suu to yet another group of educated and interesting adults.

Throughout the rest of her high school years, Suu expanded her reading interests. Along with Burmese classic literature, she now began reading books about Greek mythology and political philosophy.

After graduation from high school in 1962, Suu entered Delhi University. She still had the long thick braids that flowed down her back, and with her thin, delicate frame stood five feet, four inches tall. She didn't look close to her seventeen years, but intellectually she was years older. A childhood spent in the company of adults had given Suu a maturity that most teenagers did not have. Her many and varied reading interests had made Suu want to know more about how people formed their ideas and beliefs. Philosophy, the study of knowledge, truth, wisdom, and the nature of reality, was one of the areas Suu decided to study.

Along with philosophy, Suu became interested in studying politics. In 1962 events had taken place in Burma that would have major consequences not only for Suu, but for the people of her country, and she wanted to know more about the whole field of politics.

In the years after Burma achieved independence in 1948, the country went through a difficult time of social and economic problems as the Burmese took over governing themselves. The period of Japanese rule had left Burma with serious economic difficulties. In addition, there were many disagreements between the various ethnic and political groups.

A general named U Ne Win stepped in to try and hold the country together. He called for new elections. U Nu and his party, the AFPFL, again won the election, and he tried to reorganize the party so that the groups who were unhappy would feel more included in the government.

But General Ne Win and other military men began quietly to plot the takeover of the government. In March 1962, Ne Win staged a successful military coup. He seized power and suspended the constitution that had been drawn up by General Aung San and his committee years ago. He arrested U Nu and the other leaders of the party and formed his own military council. Burma was not a democracy any longer. The Burmese people had no voice in their government. Instead the country was now ruled by a revolutionary council with a dictator at its head.

One of the most important things that Suu gained from her studies during this period was her discovery of the methods and philosophy of the great Indian leader, Mahatma Gandhi. He had become famous for his use of nonviolent action to win political goals.

Suu studied all of Gandhi's writing and teachings. She read the philosophers that had influenced this great man. The more she learned, the more committed to these ideas she became. Their beliefs about human life were similar to those of the Buddhist faith in which she had been raised.

Suu spent two years at Delhi University studying political science and philosophy. Then she decided to continue her university studies at St. Hughes College, one of five women's colleges at Oxford University in England. In 1964 she left India.

At Oxford, Suu discovered for the first time what it

This photo of General Ne Win was taken in 1997. Ne Win's military dictatorship, which began with a military coup in 1962 and ended when he "retired" in 1998, suppressed the democratic movement in Burma.

Who was Mahatma Gandhi?

Mohandas Karamchand Gandhi (known later in life as Mahatma, which means "great soul") was the leader of the nationalist movement in India and one of the great leaders of the twentieth century. Born into a middle-class family in India in 1869, Gandhi went to London to study law when he was eighteen. After becoming a lawyer, he first practiced in England and then moved to South Africa in the early 1900s to work for an Indian law firm. There he experienced his first humiliating taste of racial discrimination. The South African system discriminated against Indians as well as black South Africans. This moved him to start protest demonstrations on behalf of the Indian people who lived in South Africa. Gandhi's protests relied on his belief in the use of nonviolence in civil disobedience.

Civil disobedience is the refusal to obey certain laws. This refusal usually takes the form of passive resistance. People practicing civil disobedience break a law because they consider the law unjust, they want to call attention to its injustice, and they hope to bring about its repeal or amendment. They are also willing to accept any penalty, such as imprisonment, for breaking the law.

Gandhi began to teach a policy of passive resistance to, and noncooperation with, the South African authorities. When he returned to India in 1915, Gandhi became involved in organizing workers to better their conditions. Then he began to lead direct political protests against the British colonial government. He eventually devoted his entire life to the cause of Indian nationalism, using peaceful protest marches, hunger strikes, and the policy of noncooperation with the government. He was imprisoned many times by the British.

Gandhi's dedication and work on behalf of his people earned him numerous followers. When India finally gained its independence in 1947, Gandhi was a main participant in the negotiations with the British. He was assassinated in Delhi in 1948. Among the leaders who found inspiration in Gandhi's example was Dr. Martin Luther King, Jr.

was like to be on her own, without any of her family. She also found a world unlike any she had ever known.

In the early 1960s, in England—as in much of Europe and in the United States—some cultural changes were happening. Young people were trading in the conservative styles of the 1950s for bell-bottom jeans and miniskirts. Rock and roll music was getting wilder. With the change in fashion came a change in attitude. Some members of the younger generation were questioning the strict moral codes of their parents. Into this world came Aung San Suu Kyi, with her formal manners, dressed in a traditional Burmese lungyi. She was naive and innocent about many of the cultural practices that her English counterparts took for granted, and she stood out from the other students.

Though Suu was deeply curious about all that she encountered in the European culture, her strict, Buddhist upbringing as well as her natural reserve kept her from indulging in the free-spirited college lifestyle. During her first year at college she studied most of the time. She didn't socialize much and she never broke the rules. Around her dormitory she was known to everyone as the "prim and proper" student.

But Suu was intensely curious about all that she saw. She had made a number of friends, including students who were African and Indian as well as British, and she wanted to be part of the college life.

She changed her long braids to a high ponytail, but it was still adorned with a fresh flower. She taught her roommates and friends things about her culture: how to wear the lungyi, or the correct way to eat rice with their hands.

Suu found that the best way to get around the campus was by riding a bicycle, something that is difficult to do in a long dress such as a *lungyi*. So, for the first time in her life, she bought herself a pair of white jeans and learned to ride a bike.

Suu's Buddhist ethics did not permit her to drink alcohol, but she was still curious about what it was like. So one day during her senior year she bought a miniature bottle of wine. Taking it to the dormitory bathroom, she drank it all by herself. That experience was all she needed. After that, Suu rejected alcohol forever.

New movements in the areas of civil rights, nonviolence, and world peace had begun throughout the world in the late 1950s and early 1960s. The Oxford students often had spirited discussions and arguments on these subjects. Now she joined in these discussions and continued to shape her own ideas and views. Suu might have been out of step with the fashions of the 1960s, but she was very much in step with the spirit of political change.

Suu dated in college, and began seeing a lot of one young man whom she had first met at the home of a family friend. Michael Aris was a British student majoring in Tibetan Studies. Michael had fallen for Suu almost immediately, but friends did not think she would ever go out with him because the Burmese people did not often accept romantic relationships between people of different ethnicities and different cultural backgrounds. Suu surprised everyone when she began to date Michael, and soon they were seeing a great deal of each other.

During the summer breaks, Suu usually went back to India to see her mother. Although she had not been back to Burma in many years, the disturbing political situation there was always on the minds

What is Buddhism?

Burma is one of the strongest areas of Buddhist culture in all of Asia. Buddhism was introduced to Burma during the rule of King Anawrahta in the eleventh century when Buddhist missionaries from Ceylon (Sri Lanka) came into the country. It became the dominant religion in the country at that time and remains so today. For over 250 years after Buddhism began in Burma, the different rulers were deeply involved in the religion, and their governments reflected this by including elements of Buddhism in the governing laws. The rulers built numerous temples, or pagodas, as Buddhist houses of worship all over Burma. The many temples there have led to Burma becoming widely known as the Land of Golden Pagodas.

Although there are also small communities of Muslims, animists, and Hindus, Theravada Buddhism is today the religion of nearly 90 percent of the population. Each village has its own monastery and supports its monks and elders. When Burmese boys reach their preteen years, they are initiated in a special ceremony as novices into the Buddhist monkhood.

In daily life, most Burmese laypeople intermingle astrology and spirit (nat) worship with the practice of Buddhism. This religion is deeply embedded in the Burmese culture. The main holidays of the country are events that celebrate feasts and festivals in the Buddhist religion.

The Buddhist philosophy of life is to reach a reborn, enlightened state called nirvana, in which a person has overcome the evils of greed, hatred, and ignorance. Reaching nirvana involves cultivating four virtuous attitudes: loving-kindness, compassion, sympathetic-joy, and equanimity (a mental balance). The ethic that leads to better rebirth, however, is centered on fulfilling one's duties to society. It involves acts of charity, as well as observance of the five principles that constitute the basic moral code of Buddhism. These principles prohibit killing, stealing, harmful language, sexual misbehavior, and the use of drugs.

of Suu and her family. Stories had reached India about the army forcing whole populations to flee their homes, and about the looting and burning of villages. Ne Win had also sealed off the country from contact with the outside world. The general and his army had thrown out foreign journalists and suppressed any freedom of the press.

Even though she was still ambassador, Ma Khin Kyi was very critical of what Ne Win's government was doing, and was not happy serving under this regime. Suu's mother would soon retire.

It was difficult for Suu to be so far away while Burma was experiencing so much injustice and suffering. In her book, *Freedom from Fear*, she writes about how some people thought maybe the daughter of Aung San had forgotten about her country. But Burma was always on her mind. She states, "I would never do anything from abroad . . . if I were to engage in any political movement I would do so from within the country." Suu knew she would go back to Burma if an organized movement against Ne Win's government were to start up there.

One summer, instead of returning to New Delhi during her break, Suu went to visit a family friend, Ma Than E, who worked for the United Nations in Algeria, a country in North Africa that borders the Mediterranean Sea. After an eight-year struggle, Algeria had just established its independence from French colonialism and was rebuilding the country. Suu wanted to see the country and get to know the people. She volunteered to work with one of the organizations that was building housing to help people who had been left homeless during the fighting.

Back at college, Suu added economics to her studies of philosophy and politics, and she continued to date Michael Aris. They began to fall in love. Suu graduated with a B.A. degree in 1967. She taught and did research for a short time in England, and then decided she wanted to go to New York City to do her postgraduate studies at New York University. Michael had planned further studies at Oxford, so he had to remain in England. They promised to write and phone each other as often as possible.

Suu moved in with Ma Than E, with whom she had stayed in Algeria. Ma Than E was now a senior staff member at the United Nations. Instead of pursuing more academics, Suu decided to take a job at the UN. It was a particularly exciting time for someone of Burmese nationality to be working at the UN. The secretary general, the organization's top official, was a Burmese, U Thant. He was the first Asian secretary general of the United Nations.

Suu worked at the UN for close to three years. One of her positions was as assistant secretary for the Administrative and Budgetary Committee, which oversaw the financial aspects of all the UN budgets for its different programs.

Many of the UN staff members gave some of their time in the evenings or on weekends to volunteer projects. Suu was no exception, and volunteered to read or talk to patients at Bellevue Hospital, a place that treats many poor people with mental or alcohol problems. These were the people that many in society would prefer to ignore or forget. But Suu's Buddhist upbringing, which had instilled a compassion and caring for all people, would always draw her to situations where she could help those in need.

Suu and Ma Than E were invited to UN social occasions, where there would sometimes be diplomatic officials from Ne Win's government in Burma. Suu's mother had retired as ambassador and returned to the family home in Rangoon in 1967. These officials knew Ma Khin Kyi had been critical of the government, and sometimes an official would challenge Suu's allegiance to Burma. She handled

U Thant, the first Asian secretary general of the United Nations. In 1957 U Thant was named Burma's permanent representative to the United Nations. When Secretary General Dag Hammarskjöld was killed in a plane crash three years later, U Thant became acting UN secretary general, and then was elected to the position in 1962. He continued in office until his retirement in 1971.

herself well in these circumstances, remaining calm, and quietly but firmly sticking up for her convictions. She was not afraid to speak the truth about the unhappy situation in her country.

Life in New York City was exciting and interesting for Suu Kyi. She learned a great deal about the American culture when she and her friends went to restaurants, concerts, movies, or the theater, or just by walking around the city. But although she enjoyed her work and her life in New York, Suu missed Michael. He had remained in England and then had taken a job in the Himalayan country of Bhutan as a tutor to the children of the royal family there. Suu and Michael had stayed in touch through letters, phone calls, and occasional visits. They had grown even closer, and Suu knew she was in love. Family was quite important to Suu, and this was the man with whom she wanted to have a family. Michael came to New York and asked her to marry him. She accepted.

Michael had to return to Bhutan, and the couple kept in close touch by exchanging letters for the next eight months. In all they wrote over 187 letters to each other, detailing how they hoped their married life together would be. Suu wrote to Michael about how much she loved and cared for him. Yet she feared that there might some day come a time when they could be separated because of her country's problems. She wanted him to know how much Burma and its people meant to her. Suu asked only one favor of Michael: that if the political situation in her country made it necessary for Suu to go back to Burma, he would help her do her duty.

After Ma Khin Kyi had retired and moved back to Burma, Suu had traveled there to visit her mother.

She had observed for herself how the political and economic situation in her country was growing worse. If she was ever needed there, Daw Suu knew she would return. But she was worried that her family and fellow Burmese would see her marriage to a foreigner as a statement that she was turning her back on Burma and its serious problems. She wanted to make sure they, and Michael, understood that this was not so.

She did not have to worry about counting on Michael for his support in this, no matter how hard it would be. He understood that Daw Suu's entire upbringing, including the legacy of her father, had made it so she could never abandon Burma and its people, even if it meant Michael and Daw Suu's separation from each other. His letters assured her of this fact.

Nevertheless for Daw Suu, the decision to marry Michael was agonizing, and very brave. Marriages of people from different ethnic and cultural backgrounds were not accepted in Burma at that time. Suu was the daughter of the most famous Burmese national hero, and would have been expected to marry another Burmese citizen. No matter what she said publicly about her love and loyalty to her country, many people would see Daw Suu's marriage to a foreigner as a sign that she was indeed turning her back on Burma. Daw Suu knew she wanted a life with Michael and that she was not abandoning her Burmese nationality. She hoped that the Burmese people would come to understand that in time.

Daw Suu wrapped things up in New York, and prepared to leave for London. She was ready to begin another chapter in her life.

Chapter 4

FAMILY LIFE AND POLITICAL LIFE

With Michael's assurance of his support for Suu and her father's legacy, Suu returned to London. She knew that the challenges that faced her would be both similar to and different from those faced by other women of that time. By the early 1970s, the women's liberation movement had begun. Many women were talking about the challenge of trying to balance raising a family with pursuing a career, but Suu faced an even greater challenge. She knew that she might potentially have to balance raising a family with leading Burma toward freedom and democracy. The day might come when she would be forcibly separated from her husband and children because of the needs of her country.

In January 1972, Daw Suu and Michael married in a Buddhist ceremony in London. They moved to Bhutan, a country in the Himalayan mountains next to Tibet and Nepal. Michael continued as the royal tutor there, and then as a government translator. He also pursued his studies. Daw Suu got a job with the Bhutan Foreign Ministry as a research officer on United Nations Affairs.

The year spent in Bhutan was peaceful and fun. The young couple explored the country with their Himalayan terrier, Puppy. They made trips into the mountains by jeep or on donkeys, and took long hikes. Halfway through the year they learned that Daw Suu was pregnant with their first child. For her, this was the happiest news. Daw Suu wanted a family more than anything.

The couple decided to go back to London so Michael could study at London University. He also began to teach at Oxford University. Alexander Aris was born in 1973, and the young family moved to a small two-bedroom apartment in the town of Oxford. Daw Suu and Michael lived on a college professor's salary, and money was tight. But their apartment was always open to the constant stream of family and friends who stopped by for a visit or to spend the night. Somehow Daw Suu managed to make meals for all their guests. Their home was just like her mother's had been in Burma—full of family and friends.

Daw Suu had put her own career and studies on hold for a while, and was busy with life as a mother. Although things had begun to change, many people

Daw Suu and Michael relax during a visit to Burma in 1973. Many people thought that she would not go out with Michael because the Burmese people did not often accept romantic relationships between people of different ethnicities and different cultural backgrounds, but this did not stop Daw Suu, who eventually married Michael in January 1972.

Aung San Suu Kyi poses with her son Alexander a few months after his birth in 1973. The Burmese culture places a high value on the role of wife and mother, so Daw Suu was comfortable taking some time off from her studies to stay with her son—although she still made time for reading and working part-time at the university library.

at that time still expected women to stay home and raise the children while the men went off to work outside the home. Daw Suu did not mind this too much, because the Burmese culture puts a very high value on the role of wife and mother. She knew that raising children was important work, too. For Daw Suu, every job done well had its worth.

But Daw Suu did not put off her intellectual pursuits. An educated, creative woman, she continued to read constantly, and she began to work part-time in the library at Oxford University cataloging the Burmese books.

A second son was born in 1977. Daw Suu and Michael named him Kim. Daw Suu loved her children and delighted in caring for them and watching them grow. She was a much more "hands-on" mom than her own mother had been, playing and roughhousing with her sons.

Daw Suu did share a few mothering traits with her mother. She was strict with her boys, and she instilled the same values of sharing, compassion, responsibility, and courage in her sons. She was always available for long discussions with them, just as Ma Khin Kyi had been when Daw Suu was a child.

Michael received more money for his teaching, and the family moved into a house. Having a house meant there was more room for the progression of guests who descended on the family.

While she was caring for her family and working on their house, Daw Suu began writing a biography of her father. Burma was always on her mind. She was frustrated that there was not something more she could do to help her country. Her father had inspired so many Burmese people while he was alive, and Daw Suu felt there should be a book about him and his struggle to help Burma achieve its independence. Even though she had never known him, she was obsessed by his memory. The stories she had heard as a child from both her mother and the general's military comrades had made him seem so real to her. In Burma, there were statues of him, museums about him, and streets named after him. Maybe a book about him would inspire the people to again fight for their freedom from an oppressive government.

In 1985 Daw Suu was offered a scholarship to the University of Kyoto so she could pursue research on the years her father had spent in Japan training for the 1941 march into Burma. There were military men still alive in Japan who had known him, and she would be able to interview some of them.

With Daw Suu at Kyoto University, Michael had accepted a fellowship at the Indian Institute of Advanced Studies in Simla, a city in northern India. Each parent had one of the children: Daw Suu had Kim, and Michael had Alexander. When Daw Suu finished her work in Japan she planned to join Michael in India. She had also gotten a fellowship as a visiting scholar to the institute where he worked. Daw Suu and Michael had worked out a successful marriage that allowed both parents to participate in raising their children as well as pursue their own interests and careers.

Daw Suu enjoyed her research time at Kyoto University. She was able to collect a lot of new material for her book about her father. In 1984, the book appeared under the title *Aung San*. In 1985, *Let's Visit Burma*, a children's book, was released in England. She also wrote books about Nepal and Bhutan for the same

General Aung San, father of Aung San Suu Kyi, was a nationalist. He learned his military leadership skills while he was in Japan as part of a group of young men called the "Thirty Comrades."

series. In 1987 she published a book about Burmese literature and politics. And in 1991, a second edition of her biography was published with the title *Aung San of Burma: A Biographical Portrait by his Daughter*.

Before Daw Suu went to join Michael in India, she flew to London to be with her mother, who was having eye surgery. Over the years, they had remained close. Daw Suu had taken her sons to see their grandmother in Burma, and Ma Khin Kyi had even hosted the special Buddhist initiation ceremonies to celebrate their coming of age. Her brother also came to London for a few weeks at this time. Daw Suu had seen little of him since he had left for college while she was still in high school. Aung San U had gone into the field of electrical engineering and moved to the United States.

The eye surgery went well, and Ma Khin Kyi returned to Burma after two months. Daw Suu flew to India to join Michael and the boys. The family settled into a routine of school for the boys and studies at the Institute for Daw Suu and Michael. At night they often joined other scholars and their families for social occasions. Daw Suu and Michael met not only Indian scholars, but scholars from all over the world. Their discussions on world affairs helped give Daw Suu an even larger perspective on her own country and its problems.

In the fall of 1987, the family moved back to Oxford, and settled into academic life there. Daw Suu started working on a doctoral thesis on Burmese literature for London University. She talked about ideas she had for two future projects: setting up an international scholarship fund for Burmese students and creating a network of public libraries in Burma.

Although Daw Suu had a wonderful family life and was still writing and pursuing her studies, she was not completely satisfied. As she had grown up, Daw Suu had learned valuable skills in the political and diplomatic fields. When she had gone to New York City and worked at the UN, she realized that she had a real talent for this kind of work.

Marriage, motherhood, travel, and academic life had interrupted any thoughts Daw Suu might have had about pursuing a career in either the political or diplomatic field. Yet she could not help thinking about her country, and the problems it faced. She knew only too well how difficult and complicated politics were. Her father had been worn down trying to unite all of the groups who wanted a voice in the government. Still, there was a restlessness in her that none of the other things she did seemed to satisfy.

One night, late in March 1988, the phone rang. It was a call from Burma, and the news was not good. Daw Suu's mother had suffered a stroke and was in a hospital. She made immediate preparations to fly to Burma. Michael and Daw Suu did not want to pull the boys out of school in the last few months of the school year—at least not until they knew how serious the situation really was—so Daw Suu returned alone to Burma. Ma Khin Kyi had suffered a very severe stroke. She would have to remain in the hospital for at least a few months.

After three months, it became apparent that Daw Suu's mother was not going to get much better. Daw Suu decided to take her back to the family home at Inya Lake. Michael and the boys arrived at the beginning of summer to find the home peaceful and relaxed. Ma Khin Kyi's spirits were lifted with the appearance of her grandsons.

A man hauls baskets through the city of Rangoon. Bringing handmade goods into the city to sell is an important way of earning extra money for the over 65 percent of Burmese citizens who are farmers.

In the months since Daw Suu had returned to care for her mother, she had been aware of the growing unrest and turmoil in the country. Under Ne Win's Burma Socialist Program Party (BSPP) government the standard of living had dropped in Burma over the last twenty-five years. The economy was so bad that most Burmese citizens could not afford to buy rice, the main food in their diet. Most citizens had no indoor plumbing, telephone, or even electricity.

In Rangoon, groups of Burmese students had started demonstrating in protest marches against General Ne Win's government. They demanded radical political change. If anyone tried to protest against the government, General Ne Win used his army to silence them with immediate arrest, then imprisonment or sentences of death without a trial. Such actions were a serious violation of human rights. Burma had become a nation of fear, repression, and torture.

But the students had grown bold because of the desperation they felt. The country was in shambles. Their protests were, for the most part, peaceful. Occasionally there was some rock throwing, but the people were unarmed.

The government did not respond in the same peaceful manner. The universities were closed. Night curfews were enacted. Hundreds were arrested and troops fired on demonstrators. Many people were killed. Those that weren't killed were beaten, tortured, and imprisoned. After one demonstration in which the army fired on the protestors, forty-one wounded students were then pushed into a small police van and left to suffocate. They all died.

But these horrible acts of violence served only to energize and motivate the protestors in the move-

What are "human rights"?

Human rights are those rights that belong to all human beings. The right to life itself and the basic necessities of food and clothing are considered to be fundamental human rights. But the definition of human rights has broadened in the nineteenth and twentieth centuries. Human rights now make up three categories of rights for all people: individual rights, social rights, and collective rights.

Individual rights are the rights to life, liberty, privacy, the security of the individual, freedom of speech and press, freedom of worship, the right to own property, freedom from slavery, freedom from torture and unusual punishment, and similar rights, including those that are spelled out in the first ten amendments to the Constitution of the United States. Individual rights are based on the idea that the government should shield its citizens from any violations of these rights.

Social rights demand that governments provide such things as quality education, jobs, adequate medical care, housing, and other benefits. Basically, they call for a standard of living adequate for the health and well-being of the citizens of every nation.

Collective rights were spelled out in a document called the Universal Declaration of Human Rights, which was adopted by the General Assembly of the United Nations on December 10, 1948. This document proclaims the right of all human beings in the world to political, economic, social, and cultural self-determination; the right to peace; the right to live in a healthful and balanced environment; and the right to share in the earth's resources. The Universal Declaration of Human Rights also pledges the rights of life, liberty, and security of person—the basic individual human rights.

ment, which continued to gain momentum. Buddhist monks and middle-class Burmese citizens began to join in the demonstrations. The protests grew more bold, and spread from Rangoon to other cities and towns. People started chasing down the police officers. Rioting broke out in many cities and towns.

Suddenly, on July 23, 1988, General Ne Win went on television and announced his resignation from his party. He seemed to take the blame for the economic problems the country was having, and he called for a vote on Burma's political future.

Daw Suu and her family watched the speech in stunned and expectant excitement. Though she had stayed out of Burmese politics all these years, Daw Suu was not uninvolved. She, too, had hopes that her country would regain what her father had fought so hard for back in the 1940s—its freedom.

The jubilation and hope were soon crushed, as Ne Win's party members immediately opposed his request for a referendum. A new chairman of the BSPP and president of Burma was named. It was obvious that Ne Win's resignation and speech were just ways to quiet the rioting and demonstrations. The Burma Socialist Program Party had no intention of giving up control.

Millions of angry citizens across the country took to the streets in mass demonstrations. They demanded a democratic system with free and fair elections, and a restoration of their basic civil liberties, like freedom of speech. The demonstrations grew bigger, and military leaders responded by sending out thousands of troops with orders to shoot to kill.

Daw Suu's return to her country had not gone unnoticed by political activists. Many activists turned to her for advice, because she was the well-known daughter of the most famous freedom fighter in Burmese history. Daw Suu tried to offer words of inspiration. She spoke to them about human rights in Burma and the need to keep protesting.

The fiery situation came to a head on August 8, 1988. In Rangoon, a peaceful demonstration was held with thousands of people of all ages, economic groups and professions. There were students, farmers, laborers, members of the armed forces, Buddhist monks, Christians, Muslims, businesspeople, artists, and homemakers. Daw Suu later explained what united the people of Burma on this day—a desire for change. "They wanted no more of the authoritarian rule . . . that had impoverished Burma intellectually, politically, morally, and economically."

Trying to find a way to reach the hearts of the military men, the demonstrators peacefully knelt down in front of the soldiers and sang a song about wanting only freedom, about being brothers and sisters. The response of the army troops was to fire on the unarmed demonstrators. Over 3,000 people were killed, hundreds were wounded and imprisoned. The day became known as the Massacre of 8-8-88.

The protests and bloodshed continued. Even with all their military might, the government was unable to stop the demonstrations. With the Massacre of 8-8-88 very much on her mind, Aung San Suu Kyi knew she could not remain silent about what was happening. On August 15 she sent an open letter to the BSPP. It proposed that a consulting government be formed that could help steer the country to free multiparty elections. Daw Suu urged that both the military and the demonstrators refrain from any more violence, and that the government release all those they had imprisoned over the last few months.

Some of the former leaders of the country came out in support of the ideas in Daw Suu's letter. The BSPP was silent. Daw Suu finally decided that she needed to participate actively in the protests. A few days later she made a brief appearance in front of the Rangoon General Hospital to announce that she intended to address a huge protest rally on August

In front of a mural of her father, General Aung San, Aung San Suu Kyi delivers her first political speech to thousands of Burmese citizens urging them to peacefully demand democracy. The Burmese found Daw Suu's speeches so inspiring that many of them brought tape recorders, which they held up high over the heads of the crowd to record her powerful words.

26. The rally was to be held on the grounds of the Shwedagon Pagoda, one of the most sacred and revered Buddhist temples in Burma.

Over 500,000 people gathered at the temple to hear what she had to say. With Michael, Alexander, and Kim just behind her, Daw Suu stood on the temple steps and gave her first public speech. She told of her decision to enter the struggle for democracy: "I could not as my father's daughter remain indifferent to all that was going on. This national crisis could in fact be called the second struggle for national independence."

As Daw Suu continued, the people listened carefully. They needed someone to lead them. Daw Suu talked about a free Burma and about democracy.

"Let us not be disunited," she said. "Let us resolve to march forward in unity towards our cherished goal. In doing so please use peaceful means. If a people or a nation can reach their objectives by discipline and peaceful means, it would be a most honor-able and admirable achievement."

Though she had lived away from Burma for many years, Daw Suu still spoke the Burmese language perfectly. She even cracked a few jokes to help ease the tension of the situation. When she was finished, the people were electrified and uplifted. The tiny woman standing in front of them had become the unofficial leader of the resistance movement. The fight for freedom was part of her heritage. Now it would also become a part of her own life.

At the end of August, Michael and the boys had to fly back to England so the boys could start their fall terms at school. Daw Suu sadly said good-bye. She would miss them terribly. But they all knew, and accepted, that she had a duty to her country and its people, and that she could not turn back. Life would never again be the same for this family.

Chapter 5

THE VOICE OF HOPE

Daw Suu began to make more speeches around Burma. The demonstrations picked up more and more supporters. The country's new prime minister, Dr. Maung Maung, could not stop the opposition to the BSPP government. By early September 1988, the BSPP government had practically ceased functioning.

In Rangoon, the collapse of the BSPP government led to a state of chaos in many neighborhoods. Essentially, there was no one governing the country. The people felt they had beaten the BSPP government. But with no government to replace it, the country was quickly falling apart.

Daw Suu joined in the demonstrations and continued to urge citizens to use nonviolent means of protest. But the people were very angry. The protests grew more intense.

On September 18, 1988, the army, under the leadership of a general named Saw Maung, staged a coup—the second in Burma's recent history—and took over control of the government. They abolished the BSPP and created a council—the State Law and Order Restoration Council (SLORC)—to govern the country. SLORC enforced the curfews that forced people to stay indoors at night. They added bans on public or private gatherings of more than four persons. Anyone who was arrested could be sentenced to prison without a trial.

Open opposition to the new SLORC government was crushed through the use of brutal force. More than 3,000 demonstrators were killed in Rangoon, Mandalay, and other cities. Huge numbers of students fled for their lives. They left the cities and set up camps in the jungles near the Thai border. There they hoped to acquire guns and rifles, get combat training, and return to the cities to fight against the army.

In taking power, SLORC stated that military control would be temporary. They said that free elections would be held once law and order was reestablished. They allowed the formation of new political parties.

Daw Suu did not believe that SLORC had any intention of allowing free elections to be held, but she still joined with other leaders of the freedom movement to create a political party. Daw Suu and her colleagues formed the National League for Democracy (NLD). Daw Suu was chosen as general secretary, the head of the party.

By December, more than 150 political parties had formed among the many ethnic groups in Burma. Daw Suu and the other leaders of the NLD knew they had to unite the Burmese people under a strong unified force in order to defeat the repressive SLORC government. She toured the country, setting up centers for the NLD in towns and cities. She campaigned to get people to vote in the upcoming elections. She encouraged everyone to push past the climate of fear they had lived in for the last thirty years. In one two-week period in late October 1988, Daw Suu went to over fifty towns to speak. Tens of thousands of people turned out to hear her.

Saw Maung in 1988, the year he led a military coup that brought the State Law and Order Restoration Council (SLORC) to power.

How is Burma governed?

After the British captured Burma in the late 1800s they governed the country with their system: a parliamentary democratic government, one of the two kinds of democratic governments. These governments are based on a constitution—a document that defines the basic principles and laws of a nation and the powers and duties of the government—that is enforced by people who hold political power and are elected to their positions. In the parliamentary form of government (as in Australia, Britain, Canada, and India), all political power is controlled by the parliament. The prime minister (or premier) and the officers of a cabinet are members of the parliament. They continue in office only as long as parliament supports their policies. The second democratic government is the presidential form of government (as in France and the United States). The voters elect a president who is independent of the legislature but whose actions are determined by constitutional and other legal concerns.

From the 1800s through 1948, the parliamentary system in Burma was controlled and led by the British government. On January 4, 1948, Burma became officially independent. The Burmese people were able to elect a Burmese citizen, General U Nu, as their prime minister. Burma's government, while still modeled on the British parliamentary system, finally became independent.

After the military coup of 1962, a Revolutionary Council took over the country and a single party, the Burma Socialist Program Party (BSPP), governed until 1974, when a new constitution was adopted. This 1974 document served as the basis of governmental organization until its suspension after the military coup of September 1988. Then a military government, the State Law and Order Restoration Council (SLORC), took over as the legislative and executive authority in the country.

Since 1988, the country's chief executive official is the president of SLORC. The State Council and the Council of Ministers (headed by a prime minister) are chosen by the People's Assembly, which is Burma's principal legislative body (made up of 485 elected parliamentary seats). But the elections for these parliamentary seats are not really free elections. The SLORC regime so controls the country that anyone "elected" to the People's Assembly is from SLORC. The leading opposition political party since the 1990s has been the National League for Democracy.

Boys help to fill sandbags that will be used to build a barricade to protect their community. During September 1988, when the BSPP government lost its control over the people, communities like this one were forced to defend themselves against theft and looting because there was no police force to uphold the law.

Daw Suu was not afraid to criticize the government. She spoke out boldly against the military killings, the imprisonments, and the violations of human rights. The SLORC regime started harassing Daw Suu by arresting people who came to hear her speak. She kept a cool head, calling on the people to remain nonviolent and pursue a peaceful means of change through elections.

Daw Suu also communicated with international human rights organizations such as Amnesty International. These groups work to ensure that citizens in countries around the world are not denied their human rights. They help to spread the word about human rights violations and organize international efforts to stop them. She also appealed to the United Nations, to ambassadors of other countries, and to heads of state, asking them to condemn the military violence against the unarmed Burmese citizens.

Meanwhile, the health of Ma Khin Kyi had grown worse. In late December she died at the age of seventy-six. Daw Suu had lost a mother whom she not only loved, but respected and admired, too. Ma Khin Kyi had brought her up to be strong, courageous, and deeply principled—all qualities on which Daw Suu now relied to face the great challenges in her life.

Michael, Alexander, and Kim flew in from England for the funeral. Although SLORC could have denied them entry into the country, they did not dare. They knew that Daw Suu's family was held in the greatest esteem by citizens of Burma. If they treated the family badly in their time of sorrow, the citizens might revolt.

During the days before the funeral, over 20,000 people visited the family's home to pay respects. The citizens were showing their admiration not only for Ma Khin Kyi, but also for Daw Suu. Daw Suu had started the movement for democracy by following in her parents' footsteps, but now the Burmese citizens respected Daw Suu in her own right, based on her own merits.

Because Ma Khin Kyi had been an ambassador, a Burmese dignitary, and the widow of a national hero, SLORC was obliged to provide government help to Daw Suu in planning the funeral arrangements. There would be diplomats and other dignitaries from different countries attending the event, and SLORC wanted to look generous in the eyes of the world. Ma Khin Kyi was to be buried in a special burial place for important Burmese citizens, located by the sacred Shwedagon Pagoda.

The funeral was a mammoth display of love and honor for Daw Suu's family. Thousands of people lined the streets to watch the funeral procession for

Ma Khin Kyi. Thousands more joined in the two-mile procession from the family's home to the pagoda.

SLORC feared that this occasion would be used by students and other citizens as a huge protest march against the government. In Rangoon, the army was out in force. Most of the streets leading into the downtown area were closed off.

Before the funeral Daw Suu had asked her supporters to stay calm. The crowds were orderly and quiet, out of respect for Daw Suu. But their enormous turnout for the funeral served as its own peaceful protest against the government. It was obvious how much Burma loved Daw Suu and her mother, and how deeply they believed in democracy.

After the funeral, Michael, Alexander, and Kim left once again for England. Daw Suu returned to journeying around the country, making speeches and gathering voters for her party.

SLORC continued its harassment of both Daw Suu and her supporters. They attacked her personally, telling many lies about her in order to turn people against her. They put up posters in public places saying that she had two—or even three—husbands. They said she worked for other countries and was betraying the Burmese people. They even called her anti-Buddhist.

When Daw Suu would drive into a town for a speech, military jeeps would drive ahead of her, and army personnel would use loudspeakers to warn people not to listen to her speeches. But the citizens turned out in even greater numbers, defying "Order Number 2/88"—the ban on public meetings. At each place she spoke, there were arrests. Daw Suu was constantly in danger, as well. It was at this time that the army stopped her and her supporters for walking

A Buddhist monk prays as he walks around the giant golden dome of the Shwedagon Pagoda. The Shwedagon Pagoda is believed to have been built in the fifteenth century. The Shwedagon legend explains that the pagoda was built to house sacred relics of Buddha, most importantly eight hairs the Buddha gave to two Burmese merchants as relics.

in the road after a rally, and threatened to shoot them. It became more and more dangerous for citizens to support Daw Suu and the NLD. Nevertheless, her popularity continued to grow.

When Daw Suu spoke to her supporters, she was not only trying to rally their support for the NLD, democracy, and multiparty elections. She was also trying to unite the different ethnic groups of Burma. During one speech she said, "We cannot have the attitude of 'I'm Kachin,' 'I'm Burman,' 'I'm Shan.' We must all have the attitude that we are all comrades in the struggle for democratic rights."

From September 1988 through the spring of 1989, SLORC arrested thousands of people for attending demonstrations. Daw Suu wrote hundreds of letters to the military authorities protesting their unlawful tactics and actions. And yet, in spite of SLORC's violent actions, Daw Suu still tried to make peace between the military and the citizens of Burma. She continually called for a dialogue of some kind between the two groups. Daw Suu never gave up her belief in the use of peaceful means to bring an end to the conflict.

In May 1989, the government reopened the universities that had been shut down since the student uprisings in August 1988. Daw Suu thought that was a hopeful sign, and expressed support for this action. At the same time, SLORC finally announced a date for the public elections: May 1990. Political parties immediately registered for the election. The NLD placed Daw Suu's name on the ballot.

But SLORC placed restrictions on the election. They said that their ban on public gatherings and political meetings would remain in effect, even after the elections were held. They declared that any polit-

Daw Suu spent a lot of time traveling through Burma to campaign for votes for the NLD in the upcoming elections. Even though she always campaigned peacefully, armed soldiers (as can be seen in this photograph taken in 1989) often followed her. Because her ideas were threatening to the SLORC government, even walking in the street was risky for Daw Suu.

ical literature had to be approved by SLORC before it was distributed. In essence, they were trying to censor any other party and prevent them from campaigning freely.

The NLD let the SLORC regime know that they would continue to defy the bans on public gatherings and political meetings. They said they had a right to print up and distribute political literature without censorship.

Daw Suu announced the NLD's plan to hold a number of ceremonies to commemorate important dates in recent Burmese history. The first of these occasions was in June. A memorial service was held at the NLD headquarters for the students killed during the 1988 rebellions. Although students gathered peacefully for the memorial, the military caused some friction and fighting broke out. One person was killed. Daw Suu accused the military of deliberately ruining a peaceful gathering.

In this same month, SLORC suddenly decided to change the name of the country from Burma to Myanmar Naing-ngan. Myanmar would be the name in English. They also changed the name of the capital city from Rangoon to Yangon. Many opponents of the government refused to use the new names.

The situation was becoming increasingly hostile between SLORC and the NLD. Daw Suu finally came out and said that she believed the supposedly "retired" General Ne Win was behind the military and all of the bloodshed. She also voiced her suspicions that SLORC had no intention of ever transferring power to any other government, even with an election to be held the following year.

Daw Suu planned a ceremony to honor her father on July 19, the date of his assassination and of a yearly national remembrance known as Martyrs' Day. Other political parties also indicated they would hold marches and ceremonies on that day. All said that the commemorations would be peaceful. SLORC warned them not to proceed because large assemblies were still considered against the law.

Trying to stop the gatherings, SLORC sent out 12,000 troops to major cities in Burma, with several thousand in Rangoon alone. They declared martial law, and set up a 6 A.M. to 6 P.M. curfew. Anyone found on the streets during this time could be arrested. Daw Suu and the NLD decided to cancel a planned march. They were afraid that the military was looking for reasons to kill people. The NLD urged people to stay off the streets. A few thousand students still tried to peacefully march to a park by a Rangoon lake, where a statue of General Aung San was located, in order to lay some wreaths. Armed soldiers chased them away.

At her house in Rangoon, Daw Suu and some of her supporters got ready to make a visit to the Martyrs' Mausoleum to pay their respects to her father and the others who'd been assassinated. A couple of truckloads of military troops were stationed in the streets in front of her house. When Daw Suu and her supporters tried to leave, the army forced them back inside. The situation was very tense, as everyone waited for the next move by either SLORC or the citizens. No one had long to wait.

The next morning, June 20, 1989, SLORC announced that under martial law they had the right to detain anyone for up to three years without any charges being filed or a trial being held. They placed Aung San Suu Kyi under arrest.

Chapter 6
SURVIVING CAPTIVITY

On that June morning, soldiers surrounded Daw Suu's property, their guns pointing at her house. Though the situation was clearly serious, everyone remained calm. Because Daw Suu and the NLD had expected that SLORC might do something to silence her, the arrest was not that much of a surprise. At that time, there were a number of people in the house. There were the other NLD leaders, about twenty student supporters, household staff, and Daw Suu's two sons, Alexander and Kim, home during summer break from school. No one was allowed to leave.

Some of the people in the house made phone calls to their families to let them know that they had been detained by the military and might be sent to prison. Daw Suu got in touch with family members and told them to contact Michael in England. Earlier that summer, Michael's father had died, so Michael had not accompanied Alexander and Kim to Burma. Soon after, the army cut the phone lines to Daw Suu's house.

She, surprisingly, felt no fear about the dangerous situation. In interviews done years later, she told reporters, "I actually felt no emotion, it was almost like I was on automatic pilot." Daw Suu packed a bag, assuming that she would soon be hauled away to the infamous SLORC jail, Insein Prison. She explained to the boys that if their father was not allowed back into the country, she had made arrangements with relatives to send the boys back to

England. As always, Daw Suu remained calm, and she helped her children feel the same way.

For most of the day nothing happened outside Daw Suu's house. Inside, there was a defiant atmosphere. The students played freedom songs and Daw Suu's speeches over loudspeakers positioned outside her home. When the military entered Daw Suu's house late in the afternoon, they confiscated tape recorders, cameras, any electronic equipment, and all the NLD files that were there. The students and some NLD leaders were taken away to Insein Prison. But most of the staff and the other NLD members were allowed to leave. Daw Suu and her boys remained. The authorities informed her that she would be held there, in her home, under house arrest.

Daw Suu protested that she wanted to accompany her supporters to prison. Afraid that the students would be tortured or killed by the military, she felt her presence in the prison might protect them. Because of Daw Suu's growing international renown, she felt that the army would not harm her for fear of retaliation from foreign governments. She hoped this would protect her supporters, too. But the army leaders refused her request. Then she asked for a guarantee that the students would not be mistreated. The military refused to give it. Finally, using a form of protest from the man who had so greatly influenced her thinking, Mahatma Gandhi, Daw Suu launched a hunger strike, saying she would not eat unless they also took her to the prison.

The SLORC military continued to arrest more of the NLD leaders, including the party chairman, U Tin U. With Daw Suu and many of the leaders of the NLD locked up, the heart of the freedom movement was taken away. SLORC was able to enforce the bans

This police jeep and guardhouse are part of the security system surrounding Aung San Suu Kyi's house. After the NLD won the majority of Burma's parliamentary seats in the 1990 election, security was tightened around Daw Suu's house.

on public gatherings and political meetings. They censored the literature from competing political parties. They took Daw Suu's name off the election ballots, declaring her ineligible to run for election because she was married to a foreigner. And SLORC banned foreign journalists from the country, so the outside world could not find out about what was happening in Burma.

When Michael Aris received word about Daw Suu's arrest, he let it be known that he was on his way to Burma. He was met at the airport by military authorities who took him to the house.

Daw Suu was in her third day of not eating when her husband got there. She was weak, but still healthy. She explained the situation to Michael. Michael acted as a go-between for Daw Suu and the SLORC leaders. He brought to them her demands for fair and decent treatment for her supporters in prison.

The SLORC leaders were worried about Daw Suu's hunger strike, word of which had gotten out to the international news media. Articles about her began appearing in newspapers all over the world. The London *Times* even called her "Burma's Gandhi." If Daw Suu died, the country could erupt into massive rioting.

SLORC finally worked out a compromise with her, agreeing to protect her supporters from any mistreatment in prison. Daw Suu ended her fast after twelve days. She had lost over twelve pounds, but gained a little protection for the imprisoned students.

The rest of the summer was spent quietly with her family. Michael and the boys were going to be allowed to return to England. Daw Suu wanted her sons back there, safe and free. Michael made arrangements with the military to let her receive letters and packages from the boys and him. Daw Suu's family left with sad, but understanding, hearts. They were cheered by the thought of seeing each other again at Christmas.

As soon as Michael and the children got back to England, however, Daw Suu was told that the Burmese government had canceled her sons' visas. They would not be allowed back into the country. But she stayed strong. The others suffering in prison, rather than under house arrest, had families, too. She and her family could also make sacrifices.

Only Michael was allowed to come back. Daw Suu's property was now surrounded by barbed wire. Army tanks and soldiers were stationed on the grounds and out on the street. Even with the intrusive presence of the soldiers, Daw Suu and her husband managed to spend a pleasant, loving holiday together. The couple didn't realize this would be the last time they would be together for a long, long while. After Michael returned to England, the SLORC government revoked his visa, too. He was banned from returning to Burma. Daw Suu was now cut off from everyone she loved most.

Daw Suu did not know what was going to happen to her. At any moment, SLORC could decide to take her to Insein Prison, or even to kill her. The SLORC leaders refused to tell her if she would continue to be held after one year, which was the length of their official detention order for her. Her life was in their hands.

But Aung San Suu Kyi refused to let fear take over. In order to combat the effects of her isolation, she established a strict routine for herself. In the first months of captivity she would rise early, exercise, go about her daily chores, and then pursue a number of activities. Later, she added meditation, the practice of relaxing the mind and body by concentrating on one's breathing, to this routine.

At first she was frustrated, because meditation was not easy to learn. In fact, the only reason she continued was because a Buddhist teacher once told her, "whether or not one wants to practice meditation, one should do so for one's own good." Years later, Daw Suu recalled, "So I gritted my teeth and kept at it, often rather glumly." Once she perfected it, meditation became an important part of her daily regimen, done for one hour as soon as she woke up. She believed meditation heightened her sense of awareness about everything and helped strengthen her spiritually in the Buddhist faith.

Her days were filled with household chores, practicing the piano, listening to music, gardening, reading, sewing, and studying. One staff member, a housekeeper, was allowed to bring her food every day,

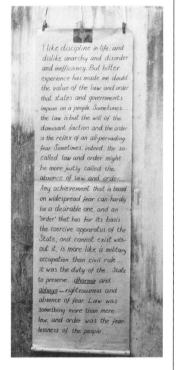

Aung San Suu Kyi hung up many pro-democracy posters that she made during her house arrest. This poster is a quote from a speech given by Jawaharlal Nehru, the former prime minister of India. His quote emphasizes that a government is ineffective if it uses fear to control its people.

and sometimes she was allowed to help Daw Suu take care of the large house and grounds. This was the only other person Daw Suu had contact with or talked to except for her guards.

After a few months the military allowed her to have a shortwave radio. Daw Suu listened to the radio five or six hours a day, tuning in to the Voice of America which broadcasts English and foreign-language news radio programs in many parts of the world where the media may be censored. The radio was her only link with the outside world.

She spent hours reading in her living room, surrounded by photographs of her family and the huge poster of her father that hung on the wall. She had used the very same poster when she gave her first public speech at Shwedagon Pagoda in 1988. Looking at his picture gave Daw Suu courage to endure the isolation.

Daw Suu read constantly, picking books from the large library in her mother's house. She read philosophy, politics, biographies, and autobiographies, as well as mystery and detective stories, an interest carried over from her childhood. Another relaxing activity that took her mind off captivity was gardening. The garden was very beautiful: there were white lilies, frangipani, yellow jasmines, and gardenias—all sweet-smelling flowers. She would go out, work in the garden, and try to talk to the armed military guards who were stationed on the property. She attempted to find out about them as people—to see their human side. Although they were her captors, Daw Suu never hated the guards. She felt anger at the things they had done, but never hate. She believed in finding good in every person, no matter how terrible their

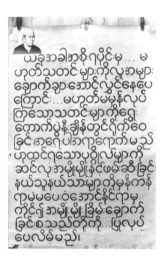

Another pro-democracy poster that Daw Suu created while under house arrest. This one is written in Burmese and shows a picture of young General Aung San, Daw Suu's father.

actions. Daw Suu believed that not hating her captors kept her free from fearing them.

The months passed, and it was soon May, time for the elections. The SLORC leaders were confident that with Daw Suu locked up and out of touch with the people of the country, her party would never win.

But SLORC had completely underestimated the power of Daw Suu's popularity with the people. Her imprisonment had only made them love and respect her more. Even with Daw Suu's name officially off the ballot, the NLD party still won a landslide victory when the elections were held on May 27, 1990.

SLORC had been defeated—or at least it seemed that way for a short time. But SLORC refused to recognize the results of the election. They told the citizens that the election was only meant to provide the country with delegates who would write a new constitution.

SLORC also announced that they could use a special decree to detain Daw Suu for up to five years. The army rounded up students who demonstrated against their actions. They closed the universities again so there would be no place for large numbers of young citizens to gather. Some people fled the country into exile, others escaped into the jungle, and still more were silenced by death. The NLD had been driven underground.

News of the election results still got out to the worldwide press. Daw Suu appeared on the cover of the Asia edition of *Time* magazine. Stories about her and the election were written in newspapers and magazines in many countries. Citizens and even governments of other countries were calling for the SLORC leaders to release her.

Daw Suu wrote to her husband and children, but the military authorities censored her letters. They told Daw Suu they were doing her a big favor by allowing her to even write to her children. She decided she could not accept any favors from SLORC and stopped writing to her family. SLORC had also allowed her family to send packages, but she stopped those, too, when she found out that the government had published pictures of the contents. Later, she gave up the pleasure of walking in her garden after she caught the military taking photographs of her. All of these were methods SLORC used to harass Daw Suu and try to break her spirit.

It was painful to be out of contact with her family—her sons were only ten and twelve years old when she'd been arrested. But Daw Suu would remind herself about her colleagues in prison. Many of their families were also in prison. At least she knew her family was safe.

SLORC became even more barbaric in its actions. They announced that Rangoon had become too crowded. What they actually meant was that there were too many people there who might start to demonstrate against the government. They said that the residents had to move to the countryside—at their own expense. For the next few years, over half a million people would be forced to dismantle their homes, move to a "new town" (usually a swamp miles outside of Rangoon), and rebuild there.

But the treatment of these "new town" residents was nothing compared to SLORC'S treatment of Burma's ethnic minorities in the countryside. The many different ethnic groups in the mountain areas had fought among themselves for years, each group

This baby boy and his mother are at a refugee camp near Nukathawa, Thailand. Thousands of people fled to camps on the Thai–Burmese border to escape abuse in the hands of the military.

wanting independence. The military had been fighting against them, and had wiped out whole villages of people. Many thousands of people had fled to refugee camps on the Thai–Burmese border. Over 60 percent of the people in these camps were children under twelve years old who had no parents because their mothers and fathers had been killed or imprisoned.

The army also found many uses for the illegally held political prisoners. Prisoners were bound in leg irons and forced to march long miles to the jungle, where they had to cut trees, remove rocks, and build roads and railroads.

As the months went by, more people around the world heard of the military's actions, and there was widespread condemnation of the SLORC government. Many countries, including the United States, called for SLORC to transfer governmental power to the legally elected party. Human rights organizations documented instances of torture and illegal arrests. In September 1990, eighteen nations issued a formal protest against human rights violations in Burma by the SLORC regime.

Daw Suu's imprisonment under house arrest helped keep the focus on Burma. The sacrifices she'd made for her commitment to nonviolence and belief in freedom gained her worldwide admiration and respect. Through Daw Suu's story, people around the world began to understand and feel the suffering of the people in Burma.

Many international awards and honors came Daw Suu's way. At the end of 1990 the secretary general of the United Nations, General Perez de Cuellar, sternly called for Daw Suu's immediate release. SLORC

replied that if she wished to rejoin her family, they would allow her to leave Burma on humanitarian grounds. But Daw Suu believed that if she left, she would never be allowed back into the country. The last hope of her people would be taken away. Daw Suu felt she could not choose freedom as long as other Burmese citizens were not free.

Because Daw Suu was cut off from everyone, she had no means of support. The army offered her money to buy food, but she refused. As long as she was their prisoner, she would never accept their favors. If they wanted her to starve, she was willing to starve. It was her own form of protest against what they were doing not only to her, but to all the Burmese people. Consequently, she had to provide for herself.

What money she had dwindled to a trickle as the months went by. Her food supply ran very low, and she did not have enough to eat. She grew very weak and often couldn't get out of bed. Daw Suu was suffering from malnutrition. Her weight had dropped to about 90 pounds from her normal 106. At one time her hair fell out, then her vision started to go bad. She developed spondylosis, which is a degeneration of the spinal column. Finally she experienced problems with her heart which caused her to have difficulty breathing.

To raise money, she had to sell her family furniture, the bathtubs, and an air conditioner. Daw Suu kept only a bed, the dining room table, and the piano, which she stopped playing after a string snapped in it. Her weak state of health forced her to give up working in the garden. The flowers died, and the garden turned into nothing more than a mud pile.

Daw Suu wrote hundreds of political statements against the illegal SLORC regime during the years she was confined. She put them up all over the walls of her front hall, defying the military. As long as she was in her house, she would do as she pleased.

In July 1991, Daw Suu was awarded a very distinguished award, the Sakharov Prize for Freedom of Thought, given by the European Parliament. The pressure on the SLORC government from other nations was growing stronger.

Then, on October 14, 1991, Suu was given an honor that was the most prestigious of all: she became the seventieth individual to win the Nobel Peace Prize. Aung San Suu Kyi was only the eighth woman to be selected for this award. Francis Sejersted, who headed the five-member Norwegian Nobel committee, called Aung San Suu Kyi's struggle "one of the most extraordinary examples of civil courage in Asia in recent decades."

What is the history of Nobel Peace Prize?

The Nobel Prizes were established in 1901 by a very wealthy Swedish chemist and inventor named Alfred Nobel. When he died, he left most of his fortune as a fund from which annual prizes would be awarded to those who bestowed by their work "the greatest benefit on mankind." The prizes are awarded for physics, chemistry, physiology or medicine, economics, literature, and peace. They carry a cash award of about $1 million and bring international attention to the recipients' work.

Alfred Nobel

The winner of the Nobel Peace Prize is chosen by the five-member Nobel Peace Prize selection committee appointed by Norway's parliament. Candidates are submitted by a number of international groups, including past and present members of the Nobel committee or the Norwegian parliament, different countries' national assemblies and governments, the International Courts of Justice and Arbitration, the International Peace Bureau, present university professors of law, political science, history, and philosophy, and past winners of the Nobel Peace Prize.

Once the names of the proposed candidates are submitted, the director of the Nobel Institute puts together a list of personal information about each candidate. (The average number of candidates is about 100.) At another committee meeting more information is required about candidates who have been nominated. It is up to the director and the advisers of the Nobel Institute to gather this material, often with assistance from the institute's library (which is open to the public). Their findings are then forwarded to the committee members for consideration. After a series of meetings, the committee makes a final decision, usually in the first half of October, and the award is announced soon after. The presentation ceremony is held on December 10, because this date is the anniversary of Alfred Nobel's death. Ceremonies are held both in Stockholm and in Oslo. Recipients of the Nobel Prizes are known as Nobel laureates.

How many women have won the Nobel Peace Prize?

The first prizes designated in Alfred Nobel's will were for physics, chemistry, physiology or medicine, and literature. But a friend of Nobel's, peace activist Baroness Bertha von Suttner, had drawn his attention to the international movement against war which had become organized in the 1890s. Nobel had given the Baroness financial support for her peace activities. It was her work that influenced his decision to amend his will and add a peace prize to the other five prizes. He died soon after the second will was drawn up.

It seems apparent that by adding the prize for peace, Alfred Nobel thought that the Baroness would receive it. But four other recipients would have the honor before she finally received the prize in 1905. It took another twenty-six years before a second woman, Jane Addams, was given the prize, then fifteen more years until Emily Greene Balch shared the prize with John Mott of the YMCA in 1946. It wasn't until thirty years later that the next women, Betty Williams and Máiread Corrigan, were honored with the peace prize.

Since then the committee has honored Mother Teresa in 1979, Alva Myrdal in 1982, Aung Sang Suu Kyi in 1991, Rigoberta Menchú in 1992, and Jodi Williams in 1997. Yet, of the ninety-seven peace prizes awarded since 1901, only ten have gone to women, even though numerous women have been nominated.

There was no immediate comment from SLORC, but the Burmese ambassador to Thailand was quoted in the news media as saying that "the Nobel Prize would not result in special treatment for Aung San Suu Kyi."

After hearing about his wife's incredible honor, Michael held a news conference at Harvard University, where he was a visiting professor. Although excited about the prize, he was still deeply concerned about Daw Suu because he hadn't seen or heard from her in almost two years. Michael told reporters that he did not know if Daw Suu was aware that she had been awarded the prize, or even if she was still alive.

"I am not sure if the Nobel Peace Prize has ever been given to someone in a situation of such extreme isolation and peril," he said. "It has certainly never before been given to a woman in that condition."

He went on to say that he felt joy and pride, but at the same time a great deal of fear and sadness. "It is a magnificent gesture, not just for my wife, but for her people. I hope this prize will help heal the wounds in Burma." He finished by saying that he, Alexander, and Kim would attend the awards ceremony and accept the peace prize on behalf of Daw Suu.

Daw Suu had heard the news of her award on her shortwave radio. Grateful for the honor, she also felt humbled as she thought of all the other Burmese citizens who had suffered and offered their lives for their country and had not also been recognized. She hoped that her honor would focus more attention on her country's quest for democracy. The people of the world might now take a greater interest in what was happening in Burma.

Wanting to appear generous to the outside world, SLORC said in news reports that Daw Suu could go to Oslo, Norway, to pick up her award. This included a diploma, a gold medal, and a check for about $1 million. Of course, Daw Suu knew it was with the understanding she could not come back to Burma. She told her captors that she would accept an exit visa, but only on certain conditions: that she be given fifteen minutes of airtime to address the country, that she be allowed to walk to the airport (nine miles from her home) with anyone permitted to walk with her or to watch her, and that all political prisoners be released. SLORC's answer was no.

When Alexander (center) accepted the Nobel Peace Prize on behalf of his mother, he was only eighteen years old. He included a quote from his mother in the acceptance speech: "To live the full life . . . one must have the courage to bear the responsibility of the needs of others."

Two months before the Nobel ceremony was held, Michael Aris published a book that he'd edited of Daw Suu's writings, *Freedom From Fear*. The book would be her "voice" in the world as she remained isolated.

Daw Suu's family proudly represented her at the award ceremony on December 10. Her sons accepted the award on their mother's behalf. Francis Sejersted presented the Nobel gold medal to eighteen-year-old Alexander, and the diploma to fourteen-year-old Kim. As he handed them to Daw Suu's sons, the entire audience of over 1,500 people rose to their feet in thunderous applause.

Sejersted praised Daw Suu for "her courage and her high ideals." He encouraged other people to follow her example of nonviolence and courage. The Burmese people answered this call. Back in Rangoon, hundreds of university students held an anti-government demonstration on that day in support of Daw Suu. It was the first major protest in the country since the August 1988 massacre.

In his acceptance speech on behalf of his mother, Alexander called the Nobel Peace Prize a reminder of the struggle for human rights in Burma and elsewhere. "She would say this prize belongs not to her, but to all those men, women, and children who, even as I speak, continue to sacrifice their well-being, their freedom, and their lives in pursuit of a democratic Burma," the teenager said.

In the closing of the speech, Alexander quoted his mother and described the responsibility that people have for one another. His mother had said, "'To live the full life . . . one must have the courage to bear the responsibility of the needs of others . . . one must *want* to bear this responsibility.'"

Chapter 7

AN INTERNATIONAL CAUSE

The awarding of the Nobel Peace Prize to Daw Suu did focus even more attention on what was happening in Burma under one of the world's most repressive governments.

Other countries did not want to have anything to do with the SLORC government until they knew the Burmese citizens were being treated better. Burma was in such a bad state economically that now the SLORC regime really needed financial help. They had to have good diplomatic relations with other countries, and that meant doing some things that would make them look good to the international community.

In November 1991, the SLORC leaders announced that Daw Suu would be allowed to receive letters from her family, but they said any letters had to be sent unsealed so they could look at them. What Michael and the world did not know at the time was that Daw Suu had stopped the letters herself because of her stand against SLORC.

When Michael and Daw Suu began to correspond again he learned of her problems with money and shortage of food. Michael wrote to Daw Suu telling her about the publication of the book *Freedom from Fear*. The book was already selling and earning money. He told her he would arrange for money earned from sales of the book to be put into a bank account for her in Rangoon. Her housekeeper was allowed to withdraw money from the bank account and buy Daw Suu some decent food. Once she had enough food to eat, Daw Suu's health began to return.

True to her beliefs, Daw Suu refused to use the one million dollars from the Nobel Peace Prize for herself. The money was put in a bank account outside of Burma, and she used it to help other people in need. The money assisted families of political prisoners with medicine and food for the prisoners. It even helped pay for visits to the prisoners by family members, who often lived far from the jails and could not afford the high transportation costs.

In April 1992, SLORC said it would allow Daw Suu's family to visit. Their reunion was joyful and private. The boys brought their mother gifts, including some new music for her to hear by some of their favorite recording artists, like Bob Marley and the Grateful Dead. It was difficult at first for Daw Suu to see her sons—especially Kim, her youngest. After a separation of two years and seven months, she observed, "He changed from a round faced not-quite-twelve-year-old into a rather stylish 'cool' teenager. If I had met him in the street I would not have known him for my little son."

That same week, General Saw Maung, who was still head of SLORC, resigned for health reasons. More changes in the country followed. The nighttime curfew was lifted. Then the universities were reopened. For years the SLORC government had been denying to the outside world that it held any political prisoners. Now they suddenly announced they would release any persons "detained politically." Over the next year, some two thousand prisoners would be freed.

While under house arrest, Daw Suu was denied visits and correspondence from her family, but in 1992, after not seeing her sons for two years, they were allowed to visit their mother.

In February 1993, seven Nobel Peace Prize laureates had tried to visit Daw Suu and had been refused entry into Burma. They had gone instead to the refugee camps on the Thai–Burmese border. There they saw firsthand what the SLORC regime had done to the citizens of its country. The Nobel laureates saw the huge numbers of orphaned children and learned about the abuse of women.

After witnessing such barbaric human rights violations, the Nobel laureates carried reports of what they'd seen back to their countries, and appealed to the world community to stop economic trade with Burma until the illegal SLORC regime restored democracy and stopped the abuses. The U.S. government and other countries took measures against Burma for as long as human rights violations were being committed.

Seven Nobel Peace Prize laureates tried to visit Suu in 1993, but they were not allowed to enter Burma. Pictured above, clockwise from back left, are Betty Williams and Máiread Corrigan (1976 winners), Archbishop Desmond Tutu (1984), Donna Anderton, Adolfo Perez Esquivel (1980), Ross Daniels (Chairman of Amnesty International, which won in 1977), the Dalai Lama (1989), Oscar Arias Sánchez (1987), and Ed Broadbent.

One year later the military junta suddenly allowed a group of foreigners to meet with Daw Suu. People were stunned. It was the first time that she had been allowed any outside contact with anyone other than her family since she was put under house arrest almost five years earlier. Everyone wondered if this meant that SLORC was going to release her.

The delegation was headed by a U.S. representative from Congress, Bill Richardson of New Mexico. Daw Suu asked Richardson to urge President Clinton to make a strong statement about the situation in Burma.

What are refugees?

Refugees are people who have fled their country, or have been expelled from it, and who cannot or will not return because they fear they will be harassed, injured, or killed. It is estimated that more than 100 million persons have been uprooted from their countries in the last fifty years.

During World War II, the majority of refugees were European; they included a large number of Jewish people who had escaped from German-occupied territories and other people who fled from Soviet armies. After World War II the refugee problem was most serious in Africa, the Middle East, Asia, and Central America. People left their countries because of ethnic and political conflicts, usually associated with civil war or the establishment of new governments.

In the 1990s, about 2.5 million Croatians, Serbs, and Bosnian Muslims became refugees in the Yugoslav War. In Africa, refugees have fled countries such as Ethiopia, Nigeria, Liberia, and Rwanda, where civil wars are being waged—over 2.5 million Rwandans were driven from their homeland in 1994 because of internal warfare.

Refugees are forced to leave behind their homes, their belongings, and sometimes even their families. Some refugees, like many of those in Burma, live in temporary refugee camps, hoping for a time when it is safe to return home. Others settle in foreign countries—including the United States—where they must struggle to build new lives in a new land.

Michael and the boys continued to visit as often as they were allowed. Their entry into Burma was always at the whim of the SLORC leaders. Sometimes they agreed to let the boys visit, and other times they would refuse, sometimes for months.

The important date of July 20, 1994, drew near. This date would make five years of house arrest for Daw Suu. Under SLORC's own laws, it could not detain anyone without a trial for more than five years. This meant the government had to release Daw Suu or try her in court that month. But SLORC didn't show any intention of doing either. Instead they announced that something called the "Central

Daw Suu always looked forward to visits from her family. The visits and even correspondence from her family were always at the whim of the SLORC government.

Committee" (nobody in Burma had ever heard of this before) had used a special decree to detain her for that first year in 1989—so the five-year deadline wouldn't be reached until 1995. SLORC had found another way to hold onto Daw Suu.

The year passed as slowly as the others had for Daw Suu. She received a visit from her family and continued her strict daily routine. Summer 1995 began and she wondered what new excuse SLORC would think up this time to detain her. She had stopped thinking about *when* she might ever be released and more about *if* she might see freedom someday.

Late one afternoon, during the second week of July, the head of military police and two other security men suddenly appeared at Daw Suu's house. They gave her some astonishing news: she was being released! Aung San Suu Kyi had been held six years under house arrest. She was fifty years old.

SLORC offered no immediate explanation for the unexpected release of Daw Suu. As news of her release spread, small crowds began to gather outside her house. The armed soldiers had left. Once people used to hurry past her front gate for fear of being arrested. Now the crowd swelled to hundreds of people, all jubilant at the freeing of this woman who had managed to inspire her country and win international renown even while she was locked away in her home. Daw Suu had become a national hero to the people of Burma.

Soon there was a throng of news reporters and camera crews in front of her gate and spilling on to the street. The chair of the NLD, U Aung Shwe, arrived. The atmosphere was one of celebration and joy. The party went on into the late hours of the night.

The next morning Daw Suu went out to greet the crowd of supporters that had gathered at her gate. She offered thanks for their prayers and thoughts while she'd been imprisoned. The people of Burma loved Daw Suu so deeply that just seeing and hearing her again gave them hope.

Daw Suu didn't have immediate contact with Michael because she still didn't have a telephone in the house. At the first reports of her release, Michael had been quoted in the British press as saying that he was still awaiting official confirmation of the news. Daw Suu was finally able to get word out to him through friends.

The news of Daw Suu's release was applauded around the world. The White House issued a statement saying that President Clinton "expressed gratification that the efforts by the international community had finally secured her release." It went on to say that it was hoped that Daw Suu's release would enable her to freely participate in the setting up of a democratically elected government.

There was much speculation in the worldwide press about the motives behind SLORC's decision to release Daw Suu. Most people believed that SLORC wanted to improve an international image tarnished by years of human rights violations. This image had hurt the government economically. SLORC wanted to trade with foreign countries and bring in investments from big foreign companies. The release of Aung San Suu Kyi and the other political prisoners, as well as the easing of some governmental controls, was a good public relations move by the military government.

Burmese women and children who are part of the Karen ethnic group flee to a refugee camp near Nuka-thawa, Thailand. Sadly, refugees have to leave many of their possessions behind and bring only what they can carry.

It was also possible that SLORC decided to release Daw Suu because they were no longer so afraid of her or of opposition threats from the NLD. In recent years, they had taken steps to strengthen their power in Burma.

Back in January 1993, two years before Daw Suu's release, SLORC had opened a National Convention to begin the job of writing a constitution for the country. The National Convention had been meeting periodically over the last few years. The convention was made up of 702 members from different political parties and ethnic groups. But it was very much under the control of SLORC. The NLD had only eighty-six members at this convention.

SLORC obviously had tight control of the Burmese people, as well. During the sessions of the National Convention, citizens were required to attend SLORC-sponsored rallies to chant slogans in support of the convention. Every household that didn't send a member to the rallies paid a fifty-kyat fine. For poor people, which includes most of Burma's citizens, fifty kyats was a large part of their living income.

The members of the convention had already adopted guidelines that would grant SLORC "a leading role in the future political life of the state" and eliminate the possibility that Daw Suu could hold office. The SLORC leaders may have thought that the country had changed enough under their control that the release of Daw Suu would pose no problem. Perhaps they believed that she would not be able to rally the people the way she had before her arrest six years ago.

But the SLORC leaders had again misjudged her popularity with the Burmese people. Instead of being forgotten while she was hidden away, she had only become more of a legendary figure. Out of respect, some people didn't even say her name any more. They called her simply "the Lady."

In the first weeks after her release, Daw Suu reacquainted herself with the people in talks and visits. Each day she would come out of her house and climb up on a stepladder inside her tall gate to give a speech to the hundreds of citizens who had come to see her. The crowd responded warmly to her jokes and listened patiently to her pleas for both support and restraint. On weekends, sometimes the crowds swelled to 5,000 people.

Daw Suu tried at first to work with the military government to restore the country to some kind of peaceful and democratic society. She said publicly she wanted to have a "dialogue" with SLORC, rather than confrontations with them. But SLORC ignored her gestures of peace, and instead attacked her in the government newspaper.

Daw Suu and other NLD leaders were frustrated by the refusal of SLORC to participate in any discussions, so they announced that when the National Convention met again, the NLD delegates would boycott the convention. She added that the people of Burma did not support the convention.

Immediately after the boycott was announced, SLORC expelled the NLD representatives from the convention and positioned armed soldiers outside of Daw Suu's home and those of other party leaders. Rumors that SLORC had begun to arrest some people were heard in the major cities.

As tensions rose again in Rangoon and other parts of the country, the international community responded.

The expulsion of the NLD from the convention prompted a statement from President Clinton and the U.S. Congress denouncing SLORC's threats against the NLD.

During the early part of 1996, SLORC continued their campaign of intimidation and harassment against Daw Suu and her followers, just as they had done before Daw Suu was arrested. Groups showed up to threaten NLD supporters whenever they gathered.

The most dangerous incident happened in early November 1996. Daw Suu was riding in her car on her way to visit supporters when a gang of young men surrounded the vehicle. Some started throwing stones, while others, wielding iron bars, smashed the windshield. The car sped through as quickly as possible. Government forces in the area did nothing to stop the attack.

SLORC continued to arrest NLD members throughout 1996. Daw Suu was alarmed about the arrests of her colleagues and the disruptions at her rallies. But she was concerned about many other things, as well.

During the six years Daw Suu was locked away, Burma had suffered greatly under SLORC rule. The economy was in a shambles, and many people were starving. And on university campuses, there was a huge upsurge of heroin—a drug made from opium, which comes from a type of poppy plant. Daw Suu knew that these two problems, extreme poverty and opium use, were related.

At least 80 percent of Burma's population lives in rural areas far from the cities, and most of Burma's citizens are farmers. These people were really suffering. Many families had been eating boiled bananas and drinking rice water because they didn't have

A construction crew of women and children break rocks as they widen a road outside of Rangoon in 1996. Forced labor, such as this, was used to prepare Burma for the tourists, who, it was anticipated, would flock over for "Visit Myanmar 1996."

enough to eat. Because the farmers wanted to be able to have money to support their families, some of them became desperate and grew the opium poppies that would later be used to make heroin. Daw Suu suggested that if the farmers had an alternative source of income, they would stop growing opium. She also felt strongly that with education the farmers would understand why it is better for them to stop growing opium. Of course, education was not easily obtained. There was a rising dropout rate from schools, and students were forced to make donations to their schools and find their own textbooks.

SLORC's rule of the country had ruined many other parts of the Burmese economy. There had been little foreign investment because the country had so many problems. Because they'd failed in other economic areas, SLORC decided to devote all the country's resources to promoting tourism in Burma. In

1995, tourism earned more than $30 million. The government initiated a "Visit Myanmar 1996" campaign. Large hotels were going up all over the capital city of Rangoon. Huge groups of laborers were out cleaning old buildings, rebuilding sidewalks and roads, and making the cities pretty for the tourist trade. Most of the labor was forced labor. And when SLORC decided they wanted to build tourist hotels in a certain area of a city, they forced residents out of their homes.

Daw Suu began to speak out against the many travel companies in foreign countries that have been promoting Burma as a new vacation "hot spot." She has asked that people not come to Burma as tourists until it is a truly free country.

Daw Suu has also called for the need for economic sanctions by the world nations against SLORC. She wants the world to focus attention on the starving farmers and other Burmese citizens, on the people being forced into labor and displaced from their homes. She has told about the routine use of torture—which still goes on—in all the prisons of Burma.

The more Daw Suu has spoken out, the greater SLORC's program of harassment against her and the NLD has been. In May 1996, SLORC detained more than 260 members of the NLD. In August, the government arrested more NLD activists. In September 1996, President Clinton signed a law in the U.S. that imposed sanctions if conditions worsened in Burma. (The sanctions were eventually enforced in April 1997.) But the repression against Daw Suu and her supporters increased. More than 500 more NLD members were detained.

In December, SLORC detained over two hundred

A SLORC guard (left) is always stationed outside Daw Suu's house as is seen in this picture taken as Daw Suu was returning from a public meeting with some of her supporters.

people that they accused of helping the student protests. Approximately 250 NLD members were arrested between December 1996 and March 1998. But Daw Suu and her supporters continue to defy SLORC. They have organized their own government-in-exile (a government that exists outside its country), named the National Coalition Government of the Union of Burma. It is based in Washington, D.C. Daw Suu and her supporters still refuse to refer to Burma and its capital city, Rangoon, by the new official names given to them by SLORC, Myanmar and Yangon.

In late 1996, Daw Suu was forbidden to continue giving speeches at her front gate. The weekend rallies were stopped, but people still gather on Saturdays and Sundays to demonstrate their support for her and the NLD.

At the United Nations in 1996, for the fifth consecutive year, SLORC was condemned for its human rights record. After a weeklong visit to the country, members of a special UN commission filed a report.

It noted the release of political prisoners, but more incidents of the serious human rights violations. In the country's border areas, the military continues to be responsible for numerous cases of forced labor and forced relocations of village populations.

Also criticized was SLORC's refusal to allow visits to political prisoners by the International Committee of the Red Cross (ICRC), an international humanitarian organization which provides help to victims of war, refugees, and victims of disasters such as floods, fires, and famines.

The UN report went on to say that today three out of four Burmese children do not complete primary school, 50 percent of the rural population have no access to safe water, malaria is widespread and is the biggest cause of death, and HIV is spreading at an explosive rate, mostly due to the heroin use. The average income of a Burmese citizen is about $100 per year, making it one of the poorest countries in the world.

Chapter 8

SUU'S PRESENT, BURMA'S FUTURE

By now Daw Suu has gotten used to living under constant surveillance: the tapped telephone, the military men who secretly watch her, and the ever-present threat of rearrest. Students stand outside her gate on security duty. They don't carry weapons, but they do now screen people who want to go in and see Daw Suu. The danger of someone loyal to the SLORC regime wanting to hurt her is always present.

Yet Daw Suu is not afraid. She has said that isolation was not something to be frightened of, and she isn't frightened of the military itself. She believes people cannot really be frightened of people they do not hate. Hate and fear go hand in hand. So Daw Suu treats her captors with compassion, and feels no fear, hate, or anger—only forgiveness.

Archbishop Desmond Tutu admired Daw Suu's forgiveness toward her captors and oppressors. Upon her release, he wrote, "She bore no one malice, she nursed no grudges against those who had treated her so unjustly; she had no bitterness." Daw Suu says that this is because she gains no pleasure from imagining revenge. Instead she gains pleasure from imagining a time "when animosity is washed away—and we can all be friends."

Since her release from house arrest in 1995, Aung San Suu Kyi has made weekly speeches from the front gate of her house. Here she is pictured with other leaders of the NLD. Thousands of Burmese citizens show up weekly to hear Daw Suu's inspiring speeches.

While still aiming to achieve this goal, she leads a precarious existence, never knowing if she will be locked up again, or worse. But she has many close friends and family to sustain her spirits. Michael recently died of cancer in England. Sadly, he had been denied a visa to visit before his death. Because Daw Suu could not trust that if she left Burma she would be able to return, she could not share her husband's final days with him. Her loss attracted sympathy from around the world. A memorial ceremony was held at her home, attended by diplomats and hundreds of Burmese people, whose courage always inspires her.

Economic conditions in Burma have not improved, and most people continue to live in poverty. Little by little, however, the Burmese population is overcoming its fear of the SLORC military government. A reawakening of political emotion is taking place, with Daw Suu as a main source of inspiration. As an old man standing outside of Daw Suu's house on the day of her release told a reporter, "We come here because we know that we are the most important thing in the world to her. She cares about us."

In December 1997, Rangoon witnessed the first large demonstrations since 1988, when the military massacred thousands of students. It was the desire for a student union—a place where university students can meet for discussions, programs, and other activities—that awakened the political passion of the students at Rangoon Institute of Technology and Rangoon University. These students had been children when some of their own brothers and sisters were killed by SLORC in 1988. For years they had been quiet, keeping away from politics. Now it was time for them to launch their own courageous confrontations with the government.

The simple attempt to form a student union was seen as dangerous by SLORC. They were threatened by the idea of students joining together in a democratic effort. It disturbed the paranoid military regime so much that it sent riot police equipped with water hoses and machine guns to stop the demonstration. Two thousand student voices chanted through the night for the right to assemble. SLORC arrested the students and closed down the universities. But as in the past, these actions by the military would not silence the voices or stop the efforts of those seeking democracy.

The NLD and Daw Suu have set up their own programs to help the Burmese people. One of these programs, the Welfare Committee, continues to assist political prisoners being held in Burma's prisons and their families.

Daw Suu also established the Burma Trust for Education with her $1 million of Nobel Peace Prize money. All funds she has been given with awards or honors she has placed in the Burma Trust to help educate young Burmese refugees who were forced to flee to Thailand and other countries.

As Daw Suu fights for freedom in her own country, she also tries to work for peace throughout the world by supporting a number of international peace organizations. She is especially concerned that the youth of the world be made to understand how important it is that the people of this planet find nonviolent ways to settle disputes.

One of the organizations to which she has lent her name is PeaceJam, a worldwide educational peace program for young people. Another peace program

Aung San Suu Kyi speaks with a former political prisoner whose injury is the result of the harsh conditions he encountered at the SLORC prison. Daw Suu has much compassion for political prisoners, and she has given a portion of her earnings from the Nobel Peace Prize to support families of prisoners.

that Daw Suu has supported is an appeal by all the living Nobel Peace Prize laureates to launch a worldwide campaign for a "Year of Nonviolence."

These groups help Daw Suu send her message of achieving change through nonviolent activism to young people worldwide. But she also has other messages for young people. First, they should not feel powerless to make changes in society and they should not see themselves as separate from other generations. Instead they should feel part of a human community. To achieve this, Daw Suu recommends that young people be raised to respect elderly people and be respectful of the wisdom and experience older generations can offer. "Think what you will be like when you are old," she says, "you will be more compassionate towards older people. Imagine yourself in the shoes of very old people and try living backwards . . . instead of living from childhood to old age."

Daw Suu also believes that all people have a responsibility to humankind. Her Buddhist upbringing has much to do with this. She believes that everyone is essential. It does not matter to what gender, class, ethnicity, or profession an individual belongs. All people are essential in their place, and all places are important. All people must have enough respect for themselves to realize that they have a role to play and, at the same time, be humble enough to accept that their role isn't more important than anyone else's.

Lastly, Daw Suu truly believes in the value of education. She emphasizes not only the education that young people receive in school, but the daily education they gain from parents, mentors, and other role models.

Daw Suu herself has certainly been a role model for women in her country. Her current battle is for

What is PeaceJam doing to help kids?

The PeaceJam organization works to address the very real problems facing teenagers today by reaching out to young people worldwide with a message of hope for the future. Many teenagers are searching for meaning and integrity in a world that appears meaningless and unjust. They are looking for people to respect and learn from. PeaceJam tries to give teens the inspiration they need by connecting them with eight Nobel Peace Prize laureates: Aung San Suu Kyi, Nelson Mandela, Desmond Tutu, Rigoberta Menchú, the Dalai Lama, Oscar Arias Sánchez, Máiread Corrigan, and Betty Williams.

By celebrating the lives of these Nobel Peace Prize winners, PeaceJam presents positive role models of people who have lived their lives in accordance with the highest principles, working to effect change in their own countries and the world by fighting for freedom and democracy through nonviolent means.

PeaceJam sponsors conferences where young people have the opportunity to interact in person with the Nobel laureates. PeaceJam also offers free educational material to schools over the Internet, as well as educational videos and printed workbooks describing the lives of these Nobel Peace Prize winners, and teaching how to use nonviolent ways to effect change.

basic human rights for everyone since these rights are currently denied to both men and women in Burma. She feels that once this goal is achieved people should then focus on the area of women's rights. She has acknowledged that women are discriminated against. There are few women working for the government, and even fewer women in high positions. But she has hopes for a better future. She points out that in the medical schools in Burma, where the brightest students go, about 50 to 60 percent of the students are women. Daw Suu's leadership position and influence are certainly an inspiration to young women of all that can be achieved. And Daw Suu herself never forgets that she was influenced by her education, her upbringing, and the role model she found in her own mother to believe that women could do great things.

Daw Suu has said that the only way to achieve a nonviolent society is for people to be educated about why nonviolence is the best way of living. She uses the situation in Burma to demonstrate that violence is not the best way to bring about change in a country. The SLORC military used violent means to overthrow democracy in Burma. She believes Burma's citizens must use only nonviolent means to win back their democracy. Otherwise, they would only perpetuate the idea that violence is needed to bring about change.

Daw Suu believes strongly in the use of dialogue as a basis for working out problems, no matter how serious or great they may be. Anything that works toward creating understanding between people makes for less violence. There needs to be understanding between age groups, ethnic groups, political parties, and countries.

If stronger means are needed against a government like the SLORC regime, it is better to turn to economic methods. One course of action is economic sanctions, where people around the world refuse to buy products from a country. Daw Suu cites the apartheid regime in South Africa. One of the reasons the apartheid regime finally dissolved was because enough people in the world refused to buy products from South Africa, and the economy in the country suffered.

Daw Suu has continued to receive numerous prestigious international awards and honors. In September 1995, she presented the keynote address, smuggled out on videotape, to the United Nations Fourth World Conference on Women in Beijing, which drew approximately 50,000 women and men from around the world. In her taped speech, Daw Suu explained that "the struggle for democracy and human rights in Burma is a struggle for life and dignity. It is a struggle that encompasses our political, social, and economic aspirations."

Daw Suu urges the world not to forget that the people of Burma want democracy. Whatever else the SLORC authorities tell the international community, it is a fact that the people want democracy and they do not want a government that deprives them of their basic human rights. The world should do everything possible to bring about the free kind of democratic political system in Burma for which so many people have already sacrificed themselves.

After she was released from her six years of house arrest, someone asked Daw Suu how it felt to be free. She replied, "I'm a free citizen but the country is not free. So I feel like a citizen in an unfree country." But Daw Suu does not give up hope. Despite the challenges she and her colleagues face, she does not doubt that their efforts will be successful. Interviewers always ask her whether she believes the movement will attain their goals and she replies, "an unequivocal YES . . . I believe not only will the people achieve democracy but that once it is achieved they will be able to make it work for the greater good of the nation."

Aung San Suu Kyi stands as an inspiration to the people of her own country and the world. Her belief in forgiveness and understanding applies not only to political struggles, but to the way people treat one another in their daily lives. Her fight for freedom and democracy and her commitment to nonviolence connect her to leaders like Dr. Martin Luther King, Jr., Mahatma

In 1996, Aung San Suu Kyi laid a wreath at the tomb of her father to commemorate his assassination forty-nine years earlier. August 1998 marked the tenth anniversary of the 8-8-88 massacre. Many supporters of the NLD were arrested and eighteen foreigners, including sixteen Americans, were detained for distributing pro-democracy brochures.

Gandhi, and Nelson Mandela. Her obstacles, like theirs, have been numerous, but she has faced them with courage and an unbending commitment. Her strength and dedication shine as examples of what women can achieve, what humankind can achieve, and what we, as a world, should aim to achieve.

CHRONOLOGY

1945	Burmese army fights Japan. AFPFL clashes with Britain. Aung San Suu Kyi is born on June 19 in Rangoon.
1947	Suu's father, national leader General Aung San, is assassinated on July 19.
1948	U Nu is elected first prime minister of independent Burma.
1960	Suu's mother is appointed ambassador to India and Nepal. They move to New Delhi.
1962	Suu studies politics at Delhi University. General Ne Win seizes power in a military coup.
1964	Burma Socialist Program Party (BSPP) becomes the only political party in Burma.
1964–67	Suu moves to England where she earns a B.A. in philosophy, politics, and economics from St. Hugh's College, Oxford University.
1969–71	Suu lives and works in New York City. She serves as the Assistant Secretary to the Advisory Committee on Administrative and Budgetary Questions, United Nations Secretariat.
1972	Suu marries Michael Aris, a British scholar. She works as Research Officer, Ministry of Foreign Affairs, in the country of Bhutan.
1973	A son, Alexander, is born in England.
1977	A son, Kim, is born in England.
1985–86	Daw Suu serves as Visiting Scholar, Center of Southeast Asian Studies, Kyoto University, Japan.

1987	Daw Suu is a fellow at the Indian Institute of Advanced Studies, Simla.
1988	The Massacre of 8-8-88 takes place in Burma. Over 3,000 demonstrators are killed. Martial law is proclaimed. Daw Suu returns to Burma to attend to her ailing mother while student protests break out in Rangoon. Daw Suu addresses crowd of half a million at mass rally in front of Shwedagon Pagoda in Rangoon and calls for a democratic government. The State Law and Order Restoration Council (SLORC) is established. The National League for Democracy (NLD) is formed, with Daw Suu as general secretary. Ma Khin Kyi, mother of Daw Suu, dies.
1988–89	Daw Suu, as leader of the NLD, delivers over a hundred public addresses during extensive campaign tours across Burma.
1989	Daw Suu is placed under house arrest in Rangoon by SLORC.
1990	Daw Suu remains in detention, but the NLD wins a landslide victory in the general elections. SLORC refuses to recognize the results of the election.
1991	Daw Suu is awarded the 1991 Nobel Peace Prize.
1995	SLORC releases Daw Suu from house arrest.
1996	The United Nations Commission on Human Rights confirms the existence of torture and forced labor in Burma.

GLOSSARY

apartheid A system of racial, political, and economic segregation, or separation used by one ethnic group against another.

boycott The refusal of a group to trade or associate with another group, person, organization, or nation, usually used as an expression of disapproval or to force acceptance of certain conditions.

censor To examine in order to suppress or remove anything considered inappropriate or harmful.

civil disobedience A nonviolent refusal to obey civil laws or government commands.

colonialism The imposed political rule and control of one country over another, dependent country.

coup A sudden overthrowing of a government by a small group, such as members of a military.

dictatorship A government in which absolute power is held by one person or a small group who rules in a brutal and oppressive way.

exile A period of forced removal, such as banishment or expulsion, from one's country or home.

fascism A political philosophy, movement, or party that emphasizes economic and social control of a nation by a government that is headed by a dictatorial leader.

interim government A temporary government.

laureate A person honored for her/his achievements in an art or a science.

martial law The law applied by military forces.

nationalists People who advocate nationalism for their country. Nationalism is a strong sense of loyalty and devotion to one's own country, putting that nation above all others and placing primary emphasis on promoting its culture and interests over that of other countries.

passive resistance A method of refusing to cooperate as a form of resistance, usually to a government.

sanctions Economic or military measures adopted by several nations to pressure a nation that is violating international law to stop its violations.

self-determination The determination by the people of a country to freely decide the form of government they will have.

FURTHER READING

Books By and About Aung San Suu Kyi

Aung San Suu Kyi. *Let's Visit Burma*. London: Burke Publishing Company, 1985.

Aung San Suu Kyi. *Freedom from Fear*. New York: Penguin Books, 1991.

Aung San Suu Kyi. *Letters from Burma*. New York: Penguin Books, 1997.

Aung San Suu Kyi and Alan Clements. *The Voice of Hope*. New York: Seven Stories Press, 1997.

Parenteau, John. *Prisoner for Peace: Aung San Suu Kyi and Burma's Struggle for Democracy*. Champions of Freedom Series. Greensboro, N.C.: Morgan Reynolds, Inc., 1994.

Stewart, Whitney. *Aung San Suu Kyi: Fearless Voice of Burma*. Newsmakers Biography Series. Minneapolis, Minn.: Lerner Publications Company, 1997.

Victor, Barbara. *The Lady: Aung San Suu Kyi, Nobel Laureate and Burma's Prisoner*. London: Faber & Faber, 1998.

Wright, David K. *Burma: Enchantment of the World*. Ann Arbor, Mich.: Children's Small Press Collective, 1991.

Internet Sites

Amnesty International
(http://www.amnesty.org)

Free Burma Organization
(http://www.FreeBurma.org)

Human Rights Watch (http://www.hrw.org)

Universal Declaration of Human Rights
(http://www.indigo.ie/egt/udhr/udhr.html)

Women Nobel Prize Laureates
(http://www.almaz.com/nobel/women.html)

INDEX

Page numbers in *italics* indicate illustrations

For my mother, who has been my biggest inspiration.

—B. L.

Acknowledgements

Many thanks to Leslie Kean at The Burma Project USA and Dr. Michael Aris for their support, advice, and essential assistance. Also, thanks to my editor, Denise Maynard, for her editorial input and research help with the manuscript.

Picture Credits

Courtesy of Akira Tazaki/The Burma Project USA: 86; AP/Wide World Photos: 35, 36, 41, 50, 54, 57, 59, 61, 68, 73, 75, 77, 84, 88, 91, 101; Bilal M. Raschid/The Burma Project USA: 25; The Burma Project USA: 26, 34, 47; Khin Ho, M.D./The Burma Project USA: 80; Leslie Kean/The Burma Project USA: 12, 70, 71, 93, 95, 97; Private collection: 24, 30, 45, 46, 63, 83.

About the Author

Bettina Ling is an author and illustrator with a number of children's books to her credit including *Maya Lin,* about the award winning architect and artist, part of a contemporary Asian American series for young readers, and *Máiread Corrigan and Betty Williams: Making Peace in Northern Ireland* (co-authored with Sarah Buscher), in the Women Changing the World Series. She is also an editor of books and educational texts for children. Ling's interest in Asian cultures is evident in her artwork—she works in handmade paper and collage and is currently exhibiting in galleries in California.